Apple of an Eye

Jane Beeson has been working as a writer since 1978. She has
written poetry, short stories, plays for 'fringe' theatre, radio
plays and adaptations and is at present working on a TV serial.
Apple of an Eye is her first novel.

Jane Beeson

Apple of an Eye

Keep me as the apple of the eye;
  hide me in the shadow of thy
    wings,
from the wicked who despoil me,
  my deadly enemies who surround
    me.

Psalms xvii. 8

published by Pan Books

All characters in this book are fictitious,
and any resemblance to actual persons, living
or dead, is purely coincidental.

First published 1984 by Pan Books Ltd,
Cavaye Place, London SW10 9PG
© Jane Beeson 1984
ISBN 0 330 28171 2
Photoset by Parker Typesetting Service, Leicester
Printed in Great Britain by
Collins, Glasgow

Sun blazes down on Ventnor yard; small birds twitter in the hedges, their beaks filled with moss and feathers; spring has come late. Old bodies, wings, and bumpers of derelict cars line the entrance to the yard, catch the sunlight and flash; the heavy granite buildings glow yellow with lichen, and tiles that have slipped from the roof in the March gales lie shattered round the foot of the barn. Cats curl against them, revelling in their reflected warmth. On the roofs white doves emerge to preen themselves, fan their tails and slither – or flutter down to bathe in the waning puddle in the centre of the yard. Dora Band's washing hangs out for the first time this year, flapping and bleaching above the old sprout stems. Otherwise, the farm lies quietly in the valley disturbed only by two buzzards wheeling and calling above a line of trees that divide the fields from the moor.

The moor itself rises stark and bare; to the north-east the conical-shaped Scarhill raises a cluster of rocks against the transparent blue of the sky, and to the north-west the high ridge of Barrowdown gives shelter from the prevailing wind but also ensures that during the winter months Ventnor lies almost perpetually in shadow. Perhaps due to this, Ventnor lay deserted at the turn of the century, or perhaps, as rumour goes, because rats drove out the previous tenants. Other rumours tell of the landlord removing the roof to put on an adjoining barn. Whatever the reason, Sam Band came there as a tenant about this time and eventually bought the farm off his landlord when the estate, of which Ventnor was a part, was sold up in 1947. He died a few years later, leaving the farm to his wife, who survived him by only a few months. Ventnor then passed to the three children, Benjamin, Dora, and Ronald, who up until this spring farmed it together.

3 January 1975

One night I dreamt my father had fallen through a hole in the floor. He was hanging from the rim by his fingers and I had to save him. I cried out to my uncle, who was sitting in the corner of the fireplace near where my father hung, but he made no move to help. I couldn't move to reach my father . . . or was it that I was afraid he'd pull me down with him? I woke up screaming.

I was fifteen, almost sixteen when I had that dream. Most of my dreams I forget but I couldn't forget that one. The light was grey in my room so I got up. I guessed it must be nearly seven. It was January and one of the darkest months of the year if you lived on a farm like we did. Even when I was dressed I still felt worried about Dad. I couldn't believe there wasn't some truth in my dream and he'd died in the night. So I thought I'd take him up a cup of tea just to make sure – that he was alive, I mean.

If this gives the impression I liked my father's company it's wrong, because Tom, that's my brother, and I were both dead scared of him. But even if we were scared of him and happier when he wasn't around, you still can't help caring about something like him dying. It's as though caring comes up out of you automatic. Anyway I was anxious as anything to get that tea made and get a look at him.

While I waited for the kettle to boil I took up the bellows and blew up the embers in the grate. Our fireplace was huge, big enough to sit in; one side was the fire and on the other a low chair. It was the fire corner my father had fallen through in my dream. I took up the fire brush and swept a little of the ashes to one side, just to make sure there was no hole coming. It might sound that I was scarey, but holes

7

coming sudden in this area isn't that unlikely, because once it was a mining region covered in shafts, and every now and then a shaft that's been built over opens up. An inn fell down a shaft overnight not far from here, so the saying goes. It's gone, that's for sure, and only a few stones left to show it was ever there.

The kettle boiled. I poured it on a teabag, added some milk and took it up the stairs. I stopped outside my father's door, my heart thumping. Half of me couldn't quite stop believing in my dream; the other half knew he'd be lying there same as usual. I didn't often take him up tea because I hated being in a room on my own with him. I couldn't exactly say why, but I did and it made me feel guilty. I thought if I loved my father I ought to like being with him. So now I knocked loud on the door and called out, 'Dad?'

There was a silence. I held my breath. Then I heard the bed springs shift. So he *was* alive. I felt like laughing. I thought I'd steal back down and not take in the tea.

'Who is it?' His shout came through the door.

'Me. Tamsin.'

Silence. Then, 'Come in. What are you buggerin' about for?'

I went in. I sniffed. Dad's room was a mixture of smells. His clothes piled on the chair smelled good, Auntie saw to that, but stronger was the smell of stale beer. I hated it, it made me feel sick.

He saw the cup in my hands. 'Bring it over, then. Afore it freezes.' I walked forward and stood the cup on the table by his bed. He took it, propping himself up on one elbow of his thick, hairy arm that was a nut-brown colour, summer or winter. I liked Dad's arms, I liked his hands too.

'Treat, ain't it?' he said, looking up at me with his look that always made me feel kind of queer.

I smiled, or tried to. 'Yes,' I said.

He drank his tea down in one and put the cup down, wiping his lips with the back of his hand. I picked up the empty cup.

'Aren't you going to kiss your Dad good morning?'

8

I dropped my eyes, I couldn't meet his. I bent down and kissed his rough, stubby cheek. I hated his beery breath, but his hair was nice: thick, not bald at all. Funny thing was I liked looking at Dad just so long as he wasn't looking at me. Even his eyes sometimes looked like they cared, yet he didn't act like he cared about anything.

'Look at me,' he said, so I looked. I had to.

'Sit down a minute,' he said. 'Talk to me.'

I went on standing there.

'Here,' he said, 'put my blanket round you.' He sat up and held out the blanket. I wrapped it round my shoulders. It was cold in his room. Icy. It faced east and got the east wind. The ceilings sloped low like an attic, and a pane was out of one of the windows. He put his hand over mine.

'You're getting more like your mother,' he said, 'a lot more like her.' I said nothing because there was nothing to say. I hadn't seen Mum for ten years and I couldn't remember her face at all. Auntie wouldn't allow any photos of her in the house, and all Dad had was a snap of her I'd found once in his coat pocket. It was a real bad shot and the face was dark, but I knew it was her. I remembered her enough for that. Besides she was holding Tom in her arms.

'Yes, you're a lot like her,' Dad repeated.

'I'll have to go,' I said, 'or I'll miss the bus.'

'So you will,' he said. He squeezed my hand. 'Do you love your dad?'

'Course,' I said, easing my fingers out of his.

'I love you, Tamsy,' he said. 'Never forget that.'

I hated it when he started on like that, he often did the day after. I got up quick dropping the blanket back on him and went to the door.

'Tamsin?' My aunt's voice called from the kitchen. 'Get out about the calves. What are you still doing up there?'

'Coming,' I said.

I looked back at Dad as I closed the door. He was watching me and his eyes were gentle, not full of the look that makes me feel funny. I do love him, I thought. Even if he does drink it's not his fault, it's because of our mother. She shouldn't have gone off and left him like she did. It's her that's the wicked one, not Dad. It was like Auntie'd always said . . .

'Tamsin?' My aunt's patience was running out.

I hurried down the stairs. They were spiral and made of granite; it was easy enough to slip from top to bottom.

Dora Band stands at the stove in Ventnor kitchen stirring a saucepan of porridge. Tom appears behind Tamsin on the stairs, sliding down one by one, yawning and rubbing his eyes. He is barefoot, and white downy skin shows between the top and bottom of his pyjamas. He wanders casually across the kitchen, whistling under his breath, climbs on the window seat and breathes on the panes to dispel the feathery tracery of frost. Squinting through the cleared pane, Tom examines Ventnor yard. Two old cars are visible, lodged oddly and at strange angles, glittering in their covering of frost. Behind and on either side stand the yellow-lichened walls of the barns, protecting and sheltering the central pond. Ducks straddle, puzzled, over the ice, and the rooster sidles round a hen, one wing down. Tom takes in the familiar scene at a glance and looks up hopefully to the moor rising behind. He would like it to be white, like icing, undulating away to the higher North Moor in the distance, for if there is snow on the ground the school bus doesn't get out as far as Ventnor and the children from outlying areas get a holiday. But today, in spite of the intensity of Tom's desire to see black as white, the hills remain uncompromisingly dark.

A cat leaps up on the outside sill and Tom opens the window, letting in the cat and freezing air in one.

'Shut the window, Tom, you'll catch your death else – and freeze the rest of us.' Dora ladles porridge into bowls.

Tom does as he's told and slides from the seat. Tamsin is fixing her hair in front of the mirror propped up against the window. Tom pulls it.

'Don't,' says Tamsin, aggravated. She takes a slap at him

and misses. He runs up the stairs laughing. Tamsin tugs the elastic band off her ponytail, ripping out hair with it, and follows Tom up more slowly.

As soon as Tamsin and Tom are safely out of the house and on their way up the lane to catch the school bus, Dora Band hastily wipes over the table. She remarks that her cloth has a hole in it, in fact is one big hole, and must be replaced. She will buy another today in Taverston, for that's what the hurry is about: today is Wednesday and the bus goes down to the market. Dora takes her green-crocheted beret from its peg, settles it on her head using the same mirror Tamsin has just gazed in, and pushes wisps of stiff grey hair behind her ears. She is sparse, wiry and wizened. Hard work and the climate have taken their toll of her, but thanks to her mother, who was a Methodist and believed in the benefits of suffering, neither Dora's will nor her energy have expired. The Bands, Ron and herself and their parents before them, have always been respected as farmers who 'keep going,' and Dora, when she has doubts while adding up the accounts at the end of each month, comforts herself with this thought. Ben is another matter, a burden she has reconciled herself to. What else could she do, instilled with a sense of duty? Ben drinks, Ben is Dora's cross. But secretly, silently, Dora adores Ben. He is – or certainly used to be – her hand-some elder brother. Her second brother, Ron, does all the work. Dora blows her nose when she thinks of her predi-cament; her mother taught her never to cry.

But Ben is by no means all that Dora must bear ('bear' is the word Dora uses exactly one hour later talking to Edith Parvey in Mabs Mellors' opposite the market), for she has Ben's children to rear. That they are also Rachel Band's is a thought Dora prefers not to dwell on unless reminded of it. Fortunately or unfortunately for Edith, depending on the point of view taken, something *has* reminded Dora of it just now in the market. She stirs her tea and relates to Edith this last turn of wilful fate: 'As soon as I set eyes on her I said to myself she wasn't the

11

one for Ben. I mean to say I knew that soon as I seen her.'

Edith, large and comfortable with sharp, close-set eyes and equally sharp ears, is well aware that this opening preamble about the Bands' meeting that she has heard on and off for the last seventeen years heralds new information on that subject which Dora will impart by slow stages. Edith knows her well enough not to hurry her, for that way Dora may withhold detail – and for Edith it is the detail that furbishes a story, rounds it out and makes it worth repeating. Accordingly she settles herself more firmly amongst her bags of vegetables and tins of corn-oil, and tries to look interested while giving her concentration to the tray of cakes on her right. Should it be the éclair or the jam-puff? The programme she saw last night on heart disease makes her settle for the jam-puff. Well, she deserves something surely after that journey down in the truck with Arthur driving wildly to be in time for the auctioneers and the ram's nose poking down her neck over the back of her seat. On top of that there was no pen left and she had to hang round keeping an eye on the truck till Arthur found a free one, so that she missed all the best bargains on the stalls and came away with far less satisfactory purchases, she was sure, than lay in Dora's bags piled up neatly by the coats. Edith mops her forehead; she feels sweaty. Her doctor has told her it is the tale-end of her menopause, but sometimes she wonders if it isn't to do with weight. No, it is probably the strain of fighting her way through those stalls without getting seduced into buying what she can't afford. She asks herself why she comes down at all on a Wednesday. She suspects it is mainly for social reasons, her tea with Dora, which seems silly as they live within half a mile of each other. Of course there are others she knows, once Dora has gone. Dora always goes earlier.

But today Dora is still talking.

'She came out Ventnor on the Thursday and I said to Ron, "That one's not right for Ben, you mark my words," I said, "she's won't do him any good." And that was the first time I seen her. I knew at once.'

Edith helps herself guiltily to a further jam-puff – she feels she has reason. Clearly something has set Dora going.

'That was before Ben . . .' Dora pauses to find the right word, 'gave in. Started on you-know-what. Ben's never been one for *hard* work, I know that. But he's strong. Oh my, he's strong. I seen him carry out trees with a girth of two foot on one shoulder. I only had to ask and he'd bring me in a log of one, lay it down in the hearth like a new-born lamb. He knew I didn't like the ashes raised, see.' Dora sighs. 'He was ever so thoughtful in his own way, Ben was. Mind you, he's changed a lot these last few years, that I will say.'

Edith forestalls a belch with her hand. She looks furtively over Dora's head at the clock. In ten minutes the Co-op closes for Wednesday afternoon.

'Now she's back down the pumps in Asherford working for Alvin Harris. I'm sure I don't know why she can't stay out the district. It would be better for all, that's what I said to Ron.'

Edith's ears prick attentively. 'You say Rachel Band is down Asherford?' She dusts the remains of jam-puff from the front of her maternal chest and looks keenly at Dora. She smells a drama. Wherever Rachel Band goes, things happen. Edith thinks back nostalgically to those turbulent days when Rachel was at Ventnor. She had been young then; she had fancied Ben Band herself though she never admitted it to anyone – not *anyone*. Certainly not Dora. Edith feels herself grow hot at the idea, so much so that she stands up, spilling the coffee of the person at the table behind. Unaware of the damage, she barges her way out, followed by the small, spry figure of Dora who moves between the tables with the neat certainty with which she conducts her life – or that part of it that lends itself to conducting.

In the farm kitchen Ben is glowering. Dora sees it the moment she comes in the door. He doesn't even wait for her to take off her hat and gloves before he begins.

13

'No one done the calves. Silly little hussy stayed out till after dark. I did 'em.'

Dora sighs in relief. 'So they have been done?'

'I'm telling you I ain't going to do her jobs. What does she have to stay down Taverston for? Why don't she come back from school along with Tom?'

Dora doesn't know. She suspects but doesn't think it right to say. Instead she drags out a box of apples from under the table and gets a knife from the drawer.

'She's rising sixteen, Ben. You can't keep her home with you all times.' Dora watches the peel curl unbroken on the table, slices the apple decisively and puts it in a saucepan of cold water waiting to receive the pale virgin quarters.

'She's fifteen.'

'Sixteen next April.'

'Then she oughter of finished up down the school and be working same as the rest of us.'

Ben's new-found interest in his daughter awakens all the old jealousy Dora has felt for Rachel. She laughs. It's not a common thing for Dora to laugh. Ben is startled. He looks up at Dora, who carefully primes the barb with poison.

'You don't imagine Tamsin'll stay working out this place, do you? She'll be gone soon as say jack-rabbit.'

Ben says nothing. He leans forward and lays another log across the glowing ashes, takes up the bellows and blows. What else can Ben, father of a lovely daughter, do? That Tamsin may or may not be his is not a question he bothers with, though sometimes it comes into his mind in the early morning when he wakes and it's still dark. Most often it seems to trouble him when a big greeny star dances very low over the top of Scarhill and he can see it from his bed. Dora, watching him now, closes her Methodist lips. She would like to cry out, 'Ben, you could have been so much, done so much. You who had the strength of Samson and looks as fine as any of them in the Bible.' Instead she cores the last apple and removes her saucepan to the stove. Ben sits back in his chair folding his thick, heavy arms across his stomach swollen from beer.

'I heard Rachel's working down Asherford,' he says.

Dora starts ever so slightly although she has been expecting this. She looks round for an occupation, something to help her conceal the emotion she always feels when Ben mentions Rachel. Is it because of what she feels for Rachel? Or Ben? Or both? Or because of what Ben and Rachel may or may not have felt, still feel, for each other? Dora is uncertain, confused. She takes down some dried mint and starts to crumble it. Ben won't eat his lamb without mint sauce.

'What if she is?' Dora finds herself able to murmur while crumbling.

Ron enters. Dora sniffs. Pig is very strong even when you are used to it. Ron draws one dung-covered gumboot from his foot with the heel of the other and walks across to the stove in his socks. He lifts the ring and slides the kettle across, then stands holding his rough, ingrained hands over the warmth. Dora looks at his two boots standing side by side. The sight of them annoys her exceedingly. She has spent her life shifting boots from the kitchen to the hall; she would like to hurl them at him. Instead she takes the large iridescent brown teapot and stands it on the edge of the stove. She sniffs again – is it Ron's socks?

'They got the machines up widening the road,' says Ron, sitting himself at the table. He looks round. Dora pours his tea.

'I seen 'em.' Ben puts his heels up on the stove. Ron's hornrimmed glasses glint owl-like as he sips his tea.

'It won't do us any good.' Dora is quite definite. 'More coaches'll come through and we'll be hard put to shift the machinery in July and August.'

As is frequently the case, neither of her brothers chooses to answer. They don't mind Dora stating the obvious but they see no necessity to join with her.

I got off the bus at the T-junction in the centre of Asherford – where the International Stores is, the fruit shop, the newsagent, and all the rest – and walked up North Street to the bridge which is just on the edge of the town as you come down off the moor. Back of the bridge is the garage where Jan had let on my mother was working. I'd thought about coming out every day for three weeks, wondering whether or not I should. Every evening while I waited for the bus home to Ventnor, I'd watched the bus leave from the opposite side for Asherford. Then today I'd got on it, just like that – which didn't mean to say I wasn't scared. It was ten years since I'd seen my mother.

I sauntered on to the bridge and leant on the parapet. Beneath me, the river was clear and shallow with bits of trash caught on the stones that pushed up through the water. No one was outside the garage; the pumps were standing there waiting for custom. I could hear someone in the big shed at the back of the concrete yard, hammering. I shifted a bit till I could see in. It was a man and he was beating out the wing of a car. I went on hanging around there on the bridge. Most of the yard was in shadow because the sun had already gone behind the hill. The hammering stopped and it was quiet as anything – no sound except for two sheep calling to each other as they walked across the cleave up the back. I looked back towards the town hoping a car would come up to the garage for a fill and bring someone out, but no car came. Bits of mist were floating above the river, grey-white like a chiffon scarf, I thought. I shivered. It was quite chill. I reckoned if my mother didn't come out soon I'd have to go because I hadn't the courage to go in. Then all at once I heard a car. It came up the road behind me. I held my breath for fear it would turn over the bridge and go on up to the moor, but when it got up close the gears changed down and it pulled into the yard and stopped before the pumps. I let out my breath. It waited and I waited. Then the office door opened and a woman in dungarees came out and walked to the car window. It was getting quite dark by now and I couldn't see all that much but I was sure it was my mother. She looked shorter than I'd remembered and more thick-set, but I guessed that was the dungarees; when you're a kid you always think your parents are tall. I crept off the bridge because I didn't want her to know I'd been watching and waiting, and walked up close. I heard her voice when she gave the change. It was Mum all right. My heart gave a bound but I was scared too. I didn't know how to speak, what to say. The car drove off, she turned to go back in and saw me. It was too dark for her to see my face even if she could've recognized me. She stared for a moment, then said:

'I didn't see you there in the dark. Did you want something?'

I heard myself say in a funny high voice, 'I'm Tamsin Band.'

'Tamsin?'

'Yes.'

There was a silence. I reckoned I was a shock to her. I felt myself shivering, trembling. I couldn't speak.

'How did you know I was down here?' she said at last.

'I heard from someone in school who lives out here.' My own voice was still high and unfamiliar.

'Come in the back,' she said, 'if you've got time enough.'

'I got plenty of that,' I said joyfully.

She walked ahead, pushing open the spring door into the office. She put the money in the till and then went through a door into the back of the building. I followed in a dream. I couldn't quite believe it had happened, that this was my mother walking about in front of me. When we were small Tom and I had thought she was dead. It was only later when we were old enough to understand there was bad women who left their children, as my aunt explained, that we learned she wasn't dead at all but alive and living up north of London. Even then it wasn't Dad or my aunt who told me, but someone at school whose mother knew of mine. Then I did ask my aunt but it took days before I dared.

My mother switched on the light and all her things, clothes and this and that lying around, made it clear she was real. She switched on another light on a table by the settee.

'Sit in the chair,' she said, so I sat. Beside me was a small

17

tiled fireplace with an electric fire stood in the grate. There was a bright red rug on the floor and red curtains; in the corner was a telly. The chair I was in was foam-upholstered and covered in a check material. Smart, I thought, not like the farm with horse-hair showing through the chair arms. I thought my mother must be earning a bit. She was lighting a cigarette. She offered me one but I shook my head.

'Cup of tea?' she asked.

'If you're having one,' I said.

She went into a kitchen area beyond. She lit the gas and I watched. She was attractive enough, I could see that; you could tell she knew what she was about. She wore quite a bit of make-up, specially round her eyes which were blue as they come. Her hair was frizzed, a bit of a mess, but otherwise there was nothing wrong with my mother at all. I reckoned she must smoke a lot because the whole room smelt of smoke.

She came back through while she waited for the kettle to boil and sat down.

'Let me have a look at you,' she said.

I didn't like looking back so I looked down on the floor at the blue and mauve and green pattern round the edge of the carpet. The kettle boiled. She went out and came back carrying the teapot and two cups on a tray. She kept glancing at me all the while she poured out and handed me the cup. I felt awkward as anything. Then she sat down with her cup and saucer on her knee and said quite abrupt:

'You've grown up all right. You've grown up pretty good in fact, Tamsin Band.'

'I've grown up,' I said, 'that's certain. Time I left school too.' My voice was a bit shaky. I thought I'd be a lot better off down here with Mum than back at the farm – if there was room.

'Is it just you lives here?' I asked.

'That's right,' she said, though it seemed like she wasn't sure. She lit a cigarette.

'How's your education?'

'Good,' I said. 'I done pretty well, one way'n another.

Got the work prize last term. Got three more 'Os' to take in the summer.'

'You're bright enough, then?' she asked.

'Yes,' I said.

'What you going to do with it?'

'I fancied going to the tech . . . if I can.'

She looked at me, shrewdly it seemed to me, then walked across and got herself a tin ashtray off the mantel above the electric fire.

'What's it like out there now?' I knew she meant the farm.

'I don't suppose it's changed,' I said. 'Nothing alters out Ventnor.'

'No,' she said, 'I don't suppose it does.'

I wondered what she meant by that; the way she said it I couldn't tell. We went on talking quite a while about Ventnor, mostly her asking questions and me answering. I told her about Dad and Ron and Tom and Dora, all the obvious things. By the end I don't think she knew any more about them than when I begun. I'm just not good at telling about people, making it sound interesting. I saw her look at the clock once and I guessed I was boring her. I felt ever so dull.

'What was it like when you were out there?' I asked, kind of desperate.

She laughed then. 'That's a long story, it'll keep till another day.'

My heart gave a thump of pleasure. So she intended seeing me again.

'Did you mind my coming?' I asked, tentative. I didn't know how to put it.

'No,' she said. 'I was planning on getting hold of you one of these days . . . only I didn't fancy meeting Dora. I waited round outside your school once or twice, but to be honest I don't know whether I'd have picked you out from a mass of kids all dressed alike.'

'You waited around?' I asked, delighted.

'Yes,' she said. 'Three times I was out there.'

I wondered then if she was telling the truth. Maybe it was that gave me the idea she was wanting me to go. It certainly wasn't anything she did or said, but I got the feeling she wanted me gone.

'I oughter get back,' I said. I stood up.

'Please yourself,' she said. But she stood up too.

'When may I come back?'

'Any time. Weekends and late evenings aren't so good.'

'I have to come with the bus,' I said. 'I can get one along here after school, but it's a job to get back on the moor.'

'You're telling me.' She stubbed her fag out and we both walked to the door. Before we went out she laid her hand on my wrist.

'How's Tom?'

'Fine.'

'I'd like to see him. Could you bring him with you next time?'

'I'll try,' I said. Something in me felt let-down and disappointed. I'd just found my mother, I wanted her to myself for a while.

'Try,' she said, sort of urgent.

'All right,' I said, unwilling.

She must have sensed I was feeling bad because she leant forward and kissed me on the cheek.

'My Tamsin,' she said. 'I can't believe it. After ten years.'

'Yes.' I said.

I walked up to the bus-stop light footed. I felt like a new person. There was something about my mother that excited me; it was as though she was living and all of us out on the farm were half dead. She made me think she knew things my aunt wouldn't ever let on she knew even if she did. What stuck in my mind most was Mum's independence – all the years I'd held it against her for leaving Tom and me I forgave. I thought that my mum was more of a person than my aunt, who scraped and nagged and reared us in spite of everything. I don't know if I'd think the same now, but now's different. I'm talking about then.

One thing I did know was I wanted to see her again, and soon. Tom was the problem. I didn't fancy telling Tom in case he came out with it, told the rest. Or that's what I told myself. I could bribe him to keep his mouth shut, I thought, but you never knew with Tom. By the time the bus came I'd decided I'd forget about him and maybe my mother would too.

Up on top the moor it was a lot colder. I looked out the windows down across the lights of the valley towns by the sea, or where I knew the sea was, because there wasn't a moon. The ports looked big at night. Riding along in the bus looking down over I got that same little shiver I got with Mum, like there was lots going on I didn't know about, another world. I pulled my knees up on the seat and hugged them.

Back at Ventnor I slipped in the back and went upstairs. I wanted to be by myself to think about my mother, about her life down there and what she must have thought of me. I drew the curtains and switched on the table lamp. Then I sat down and looked at myself a long time in the spotted mirror on the dressing-table, trying hard to see what I must have looked like to Mum. My face was oval, same as the mirror, my skin was quite pale – sallow my aunt said – and my eyes were big and dark. I was pleased with them. My hair looked black as anything in this light but I knew for a fact it was only dark brown. After a bit I stopped seeing my face and went back to seeing that small square room with the telly in the corner and my mother getting up off the settee to fetch the tin ashtray. I wondered why it was that particular thing she'd done had stuck in my mind. Probably it was to do with something she'd said but I couldn't remember what, so I gave up trying and started doing my hair different ways. I always came back to the first: parted in the middle, the top part drawn back by a slide and the rest hanging down straight. They didn't fuss about it at school if I wore it that way.

Then I lay down on my bed and tried to do my

homework, but too much else was going round in my mind. I went downstairs. I was hungry.

Rachel Band presses the last of her ash into the tin tray and folds her arms. If she folds them it will stop her fidgeting with her hands and that will make her feel calmer. She is waiting for Joe, who is working on the new motorway. Joe is fifteen years younger than herself – a fact of which Rachel is overconscious. She also feels flattered for surely, she reasons, it must mean she has retained her looks and is still attractive. Or is it just sex? She feels depressed at the last thought; she would so much like to be more than sexy. Many years ago she became disillusioned about her sex and decided any woman is sexy when a man happens to feel like it. At school she had always thought 'sex appeal' was something special, had even felt pleased if her friends accused her of 'being sexy'. Now she sees things differently, she sees them as they are. Largely, she feels, sex is a question of being available. For a woman. She would give a lot to try being a man. She is pretty sure they get more fun out of it . . . in the end. It stands to reason, doesn't it; they are keener, more desperate and all that.

In spite of disparaging sex Rachel has no qualms about using it when necessary, and that has been quite often since she left Ben. Not that she regrets leaving Ben, or does she? Sometimes she wonders. She pushes her hair back off her forehead and examines a small rash of pink spots. Perhaps they are a sign of youthful hormones. Like teenagers. Rachel is optimistic. It is her optimism that has stood by her these last ten years, or nine. A year ago things took a turn for the better. She met Arthur Prenn, the garage owner, through usual means – a friend introduced her to a friend, who introduced her to Arthur. They had an affair. Arthur ran off with someone else, sold up and left Rachel to work for the next owner. Which is better altogether, Rachel has long since decided, because now she works with no strings attached whereas with Arthur it had got to be a bind. It is only in the last few months she has met Joe and it has proved a mixed blessing. Usually Rachel discusses men with Donna Barker, who works in The Lion, but with Joe being so much younger Rachel prefers to keep it to herself. She's not sure what others will think, even Donna, who is very broad-minded. So Rachel endures her suffering – for it is mainly suffering – on her own. She wonders now, as she looks at the clock, how much more suffering she can bear. She has not had a Methodist upbringing, in fact she has had very little upbringing at all. Her mother brought her fifteen years ago to Devon on a coach trip and Rachel met Ben in The Fox down Poundford. Her mother left Rachel behind thankfully and returned to the other five in Wigan. Rachel often ponders whether her mother meant to dispose of her that trip or whether it was accidental. She has been back to see her mother twice since but hesitates to ask.

Rachel is thirty-eight but looks more and, worse still, feels more. It is her life, her friends tell her. Rachel takes them to mean it has been hard. She chews round the edges of her fingers as she waits for Joe and again looks at the clock. She thinks for a moment she hears his motorbike and hurries across to the window. No. She lights another cigarette and allows herself to indulge in the imaginary luxury of sharing her suffering with Donna. For, the minute you tell someone else, suffering is transformed; love-suffering anyway, and fortunately Rachel hasn't had much else. Except a bit of poverty, but Rachel is used to that. She reckons no one is poor south of London, they should see what it's like up in the North; anyway no one is *really* poor with a welfare state. Her father taught her that before he died. He'd lived through the 1930s depression.

Lights of a bike flash through the lace curtains. Rachel starts up like a rabbit. No. The engine fades as it roars on up the hill. Rachel sinks back into the delicious indulgence of her masochistic fantasy:

Donna: 'I can't see what you see in 'im, Rach. He's a good looker, I know that. His eyes – phew! Set me heart beating. But he don't have nothing to say as far as I can see. What do you *talk* about all the time?'

Rachel: 'We don't talk. I don't like him for his conversation. It's the other. You can't imagine if you never had it. I couldn't imagine it before, not even with Ben. I'm telling you, you don't know what it's like.'

Donna (put out): 'I'm sure I've had good as you can get from Sid. I don't know where I'd find better.'

Rachel: 'I think sometimes I'm one of the lucky ones. I've been given a special experience. Of love. I truly love Joe, Donna. It's the first time I've loved anyone proper.'

Donna (wishing to deflate): 'It can't last – not with you in your late thirties and him not turned twenty.'

Rachel enjoys this last self-inflicted thrust. She gives a little moan of anguish and stuffs some of her pillow thoughtfully brought through on to the settee into her mouth. Will Joe never come?

Then a small frown creases her forehead. She sits up and bites more fiercely at the sides of her nails. She is thinking about Tamsin. What shall she do about Tamsin? Should she or shouldn't she allow Tamsin to know about Joe? More to the point, how is she to prevent Tamsin finding out about Joe? Rachel tries, very briefly, to examine her feelings for her new-found daughter. She must, after all, love her, mustn't she? Certainly. But just now, in the midst of Joe, it is very inconvenient. Tamsin has been to see her twice since that first time, and it is disconcerting never knowing when she may turn up. She rather expected her this evening, in fact she told Joe not to come till late because of it, and now look what has happened. Joe hasn't come at all. Rachel looks yet again at the clock. Bugger it, she thinks. Bugger Tamsin, Joe; bugger all of them. She would like to bust up the room, smash the clock and run off for ever. Let them miss her for once. She's too reliable, that's the trouble. Slowly she unzips her dress and lets it slip down over her enticingly clad, but solid, frame. She gets into bed. It's midnight. Joe never comes after eleven. She slithers into the cold, lonely sheets and buries her face under the quilt. She'll never sleep. She sits up and takes some aspirins, gives up all hope of love and falls asleep.

Through her window the stars shoot across the sky for no reason and the Milky Way drifts mazily above Joe standing in Fore Street with his Triumph propped up against him, kissing Diane.

'You'll have to improve on this, if you're going to pass,' she said.

I despaired of improving. I'd tried as hard as I could. Or had I? Maybe I hadn't concentrated all that well, I'd got other things to think about. I was planning on going down for a weekend with my mum if she'd have me. In fact I was going along there now.

I grabbed back my essay from Miss Jennings and ran out the building, just in time for the Asherford bus, thank my lucky stars! Twenty minutes later I was walking up the road to Asherford filling station feeling nervous at the thought of seeing Mum. I don't know why I felt like I did, but that's how it was. I couldn't be quite natural with her. I was always putting on an act; I didn't *mean* to, I couldn't help it. I wondered if she knew the person she met out at the garage wasn't the same as the one I was back at the farm. The one at the farm was me, I knew that. I was shy of her, that was the trouble. I wanted her to think me better than I was.

I came round the corner and there she was talking to a young bloke outside the office. I hesitated. He looked my way, said something to my mother, crossed the yard and got on his motorbike. Two moments later the engine was roaring, he fastened his helmet, wheeled round past me and was gone. When I looked back at Mum, she was bending down examining an inner tube. As I went up she laid it on one side and straightened up.

'Tamsin.'
'Hullo.'
Bit of a silence.
'Thought I'd come along.'
'Fine.'
Yet I felt she wasn't pleased.
'I'll keep out the way till you've finished,' I said.

'I'm finished now,' she said. 'We'll go in.'

She led the way as usual into that small back room I'd grown familiar with – this was the fourth time. I dropped my satchel and sat on the yellow leather chair in front of the telly. Mum sat on the chair opposite. She looked a bit different to usual though I couldn't tell exactly why. Then I saw it was her eyebrows, she'd plucked them; it made her look permanently surprised. She didn't seem so easy as usual and because of that I was edgy too.

'Tell me about the farm,' she said sudden. 'How's all of them?'

'My aunt's always busy,' I said. 'So's Ron. Dad doesn't do so much.'

'Don't you get on with him, your dad?'

'No,' I said. 'I can't abide him.'

She looked at me curiously but didn't say anything. Now we'd got so far I thought I might as well come out with it.

'I planned on coming this next weekend like you suggested.'

She frowned. 'This coming one?'

'Yes,' I said.

She seemed uncertain. 'I won't come if it doesn't suit,' I said quick.

She looked out the window a moment, then seemed to make up her mind. 'Make it the one after,' she said. 'It would suit me better.'

I felt she must see disappointment all over my face though I tried to hide it.

'Whatever you think's best,' I said.

'I've got more free time next weekend,' she said. 'This one I'm working all through Saturday.'

'OK. Next,' I said.

And that's how we left it.

I spent the rest of the week worrying. Did my mother want me at all? Did she like me even? Why hadn't she wanted me last weekend? Was it because I hadn't taken Tom down? I didn't get much work done at school and I kept out the way back at the farm till the Thursday when I had to come down and tell them.

'I'm going to stay down Asherford with Denise for the weekend,' I said.

My aunt looked up.

'Denise? Denise who?'

'Denise Bawden,' I said. 'The one I go along and see some evenings.' My aunt went on with her hooking. Dad looked over to me.

'I says, no,' he said.

'Why can't I?'

'While I'm looking after you, providing you with board and keep, this is where you'll come to in your leisure time. Right back under my roof.'

'But Dad . . .' I said.

'Dora needs help,' he said. 'And you're the one to give it. The Bawdens ain't no friends of mine anyways.'

Ron looked up from the *Advertiser* he had spread on the table.

'I thought the Bawdens had left Asherford. Gone down Lanacombe?' He goggled through his spectacles. Nine times out of ten he wouldn't have talked. He hardly ever said anything except about the weather, the animals or money.

'They're thinking about it,' I said. 'But they haven't gone.' I turned to Dad. 'Please, Dad,' I said, 'let me go this once. She's having a party on Saturday and I won't be able to get back up here late at night.'

Silence. Then Dora said:

'Let her go, Ben. I can manage on me own same as I always have.' She always liked to make herself out a martyr.

I felt like standing up and shouting at Dad, 'You'll be out drinking tomorrow, like as not, and won't know whether I'm here or gone.' But I knew that wouldn't help me get my way. Also I didn't dare. There were a lot of things I didn't dare when Dad was around – I suppose I was afraid of making him angry. When he was angry the whole of me shook, every inch of me twanged and jarred, I wanted to cry for hating him. That's how he worked on me. He was the one could upset me. So I spent most of my time trying not to cross him, keeping out the way. But sometimes, like now, I couldn't avoid it.

'If Dora says you can go, then I ain't one to interfere,' he said. 'But you'll be back to do the calves.'

'I'm away the *night*, Dad,' I said. 'How can I do 'em?'

'You'll see to it they're done.' He glowered at me.

'Tom'll do them,' I said. 'I'll ask Tom.'

Dad shut his eyes. The clock ticked. Dora pulled at her mat, a piece of wool in her mouth. I closed up my books, stood up, went to the door.

'Tamsin?' – it was my father's voice.

I started as though I'd been shot in the back. I didn't turn round.

'Yes?'

'Come and say goodnight.'

I turned and went slowly back across the room. I bent forward and pressed my lips against the coarse red-black skin of my father's face. He smelt of tobacco and animals. I didn't mind the smell.

'The other one.'

I walked over his stretched legs and kissed the other cheek, hot from the fire. He reached up his hand and pulled down my neck, forcing my mouth towards his own. I couldn't bear it. I pulled away.

'That wasn't much of a kiss,' he said.

Desperate, I kissed him again on his lips. Then it was over and I went once more to the door.

'Goodnight Dora,' I said.

'Aunt,' said my father.

'I told her *Dora*'s enough now she's grown.' Dora took the wool out of her mouth. I felt a bit odd saying it: *Dora* on its own is sort of short and naked. Naked? I wondered about that. Was my aunt ever rounded out, like me, or was she always a stick? Just the opposite to Mum. Perhaps she never married because she was a stick, or perhaps she grew into a stick because she never married. I went up the stairs wondering, then my mind turned to tomorrow. I started thinking what I should wear. I liked looking good for Mum. I wanted her to be proud of me.

Tom came in when I was undressing. He opened the door as though it was opening on its own, or by a ghost.

'I'm undressing,' I said.

He came in.

'You're getting fatter,' he said, staring at me critical.

'Shut up and mind your own business.'

I was hopping about getting out of my tights. I remembered I'd got to be good to Tom.

'Will you do the calves tomorrow and Saturday?' I asked.

'Shit an' I will.'

'Go on,' I said. 'Do something for me for once.'

'You'll have to pay,' he said, cool as anything.

He sat on the foot of my bed.

'I'll get the lamp for your bike,' I said.

'Promise?'

'If you do them *both* nights.'

'What about mornings?'

'She'll do 'em.'

A long pause while I got my nightshirt over my head. I tugged it down and got in the freezing sheets.

'Will you . . . Tom?' I was pleading to my younger brother. 'Please.'

'I want one battery in the lamp and another spare.'

'OK,' I said.

He went on sitting there. I wished he'd go. I liked him but he was a pest.

'Where are you going, then?'

'Down Asherford.'

'Where?'

'Stay with Denise.'

'Come off it!'

At last I said it.

'Stay with our mum.'

Tom stared at me.

'You're joking?'

'No.'

'Where to?'

'Down the petrol station.'

'Serious?'

'Course I am.'

'Shit.' He was silent for a bit. Then, 'How come you're going to stay?'

'She asked me.'

He looked a bit forlorn, so I said, 'She wants to see you sometime, too.'

His lips pouted. I could see he was thinking a lot of things he wasn't saying.

'I could come along, I suppose,' he said. I knew it was curiosity, but then what else could a kid left at three years old feel?

'OK,' I said. 'I'll take you another time. But keep quiet about it or there won't be no other time.' I could see he was going to keep on questioning me and I wanted some peace. So I told him to go. He got up and walked off silly with his toes turned in. He closed the door, but it opened again.

'Shut the door,' I shouted.

He didn't. I got out swearing and banged it shut.

Ron comes across the yard, carrying milk for the house. Halfway he pauses and looks up at the hill in front of him: Scarhill. The light behind the dark line of its edge is white, transparent white, it slides off into pink, then grey. It means a lot to Ron, this light. On a fine evening he looks forward to seeing it, even now at only four o'clock when the shaded sides of the buildings are still white from frost the night before, even in the bitter cold of the shaded yard he stops to look at Scarhill. Barrowdown's behind him, high and long; it's the one that breaks the clouds, meets the weather. But Scarhill is the one Ron knows, watches, not only for his sheep and ponies that graze up there, but because it fills his soul, that bit of him you can't touch, fills it in a way he's never known it filled by chapel in spite of going regularly with Dora. Ron places the bucket down and scratches the back of his rough, red neck, then picks it up and walks into the house through the covered alley to the back door. He tips the milk into a bowl standing on the slate slab in the dairy, places the bucket under the cold water tap, and goes into the kitchen.

Dora hasn't lit the fire, she's too busy. A tatty velvet curtain is nailed across the fireplace to prevent cold air being sucked down. Ron crosses to the stove and warms his hands. He wonders what's the matter with Dora. He'd like a fire.

'Where's Ben?'

'I don't know where he's to, but I know where he's a-heading for.'

So does Ron. He wonders if he himself may not be heading for the same place. He wipes his nose on the back of his hand – it always drips in cold weather.

'Tea?'

'Put the kettle over. I've only got one pair of hands.' Ron does as he's told. It's not the moment to cross Dora. Any minute now the trouble will eject like someone being sick. It's not a nice simile but watching Dora doesn't send nice similes through Ron's head. In fact, Ron is the only one in the house other than Tamsin who knows what a simile is, because Ron reads. All those long evenings, before Dora allowed them to spend on a television, Ron read. Ron had a good education at a small day-school years back; so did Ben and Dora. But Ben wasn't the kind to learn, he was too athletic, and Dora wasn't keen on learning if it led her away from the Bible. Dora was good at sums and that is how it has stayed. Dora keeps the accounts, Ron works and Ben . . . lives. Ron hesitates for some seconds before he settles for this verb. He has a penchant for accuracy, a leaning for words. Though he speaks a local dialect, he thinks in exact English, or so he believes. He wipes his nose again and pours the boiling water on the three Tetley teabags he's placed in the pot. He had tea once with Angela Barnett,

31

two farms down the valley; it was jasmin served with lemon. Ron hankers now for delicate jasmin as he removes the teabags by their strings.

Dora sits down the opposite side of the table to Ron and pulls a cup towards her. Ron fills it. His leathery hands ingrained with dirt, his broken nails, do nothing to spoil the steadiness with which the brown water pours from the heavy pot into the clumsy cup. Dora adds milk and sugar and takes up her cup. She sips.

Ron drinks from his own, conscious of the weighty gulp he makes as the tea passes down his throat. He felt embarrassed at Angela Barnett's, he remembers. Now he feels a pleasant sense of relaxation; there is no need for niceties in front of Dora. He belches.

Dora frowns. Ron thinks it's the belch but in fact it is because Tamsin is on her mind. Her frown grows deeper. Can it be that Tamsin has been seeing her mother? Resentment and jealousy set to work in Dora at the very thought. She has brought up Tamsin and Tom. Rachel has no right to them. She says as much.

Ron drinks his tea and tries to concentrate. Nothing annoys Dora more than people who don't listen when she is worked up. Ron looks furtively over his cup. Dora is looking at him, waiting for an answer.

'I heard a couple of months back she was working down there,' Ron admits.

'Then why didn't you say?' Dora asks sharply. 'Why is it I'm always left to hear what concerns mine from others?'

Ron can't answer. It seems to him quite natural. It is the way news usually passes round in the country. Most people, he has found, know what they will do before he knows it himself. It doesn't worry Ron; he finds it helps him to make up his mind, a thing he hates doing.

Dora hasn't finished.

'If Tamsin's been along of Rachel I can't see much help for her, I don't know why Rachel has to come back this way, I'm sure. I thought she'd gone up country, that's what I heard.'

32

Ron stares, puzzled, at Dora.

'I thought you was the one gave her permission to go down Asherford this weekend?'

'I can't keep the girl as though she's in prison, can I?'

Dora would certainly like to, it seems to Ron.

'You could have told her to keep away from Rachel.'

'She's Ben's girl, not mine.'

'I thought Ben was for keeping her back.' Ron's confusion grows.

Dora is exasperated.

'It's not a question of forcing – it's what she chooses. If she wants to see Rachel then I'm not one to stop her. But I should'a thought after all these years of me raising her, and her mother up and leaving her like she done, that Tamsin might'a given a thought to me before she gone down Rachel's.'

Ron blinks. He doesn't like it when Dora gets emotional. Everything indicates she will shortly blow her nose, which in Dora's case means crying. He looks round for a means of escape. His eyes light on the television.

'Well what do you suggest?'

Ron, halfway to the television, is not sure what Dora would like him to suggest. If he was he would willingly suggest it.

'Ben could go and ask Rachel to let her be,' he says. At the same time he turns on the switch; full, so the volume will come up loud. Dora is enraged as he has feared she may be.

'None of you give me any help. None of you care two pins for anyone except you and yours . . .' Dora blows her nose at the same moment as the television comes up. Ron, under the pretext of not hearing, pulls his chair up and faces it. Dora leaves the kitchen, taking Ron's gumboots with her. She flings them outside the back door to fill with snow she hopes.

In the night she wakes up conscience-stricken. She creeps down the stone spiral, opens the door on the freezing, crisp and uneven ground and pulls in the boots.

She stands them to warm by the stove. On the way back up the stairs she sniffs. Pig. She goes to the bathroom to wash her hands. She comforts herself that the bacon they had from the last one lasted six months.

On the Friday afternoon we had a sponsored walk so it wasn't difficult for me to slip off early. There was no bus so I hitched and got to Asherford by three thirty. Mum wasn't expecting me till five, the usual time for the bus. I thought she'd still be out the pumps and maybe I could give her a hand. But no, the only one around was Alf, the old bloke who filled in when Mum was gone or when there was a lot of traffic like Whitsun and bank holidays. He nodded to me because he'd seen me often enough before. I nodded and went on through the back. Still no sign of Mum. I guessed she was down the shops or something. Maybe she was even buying food, though that didn't seem likely. Mum lived out of tins – baked beans, sardines, tomatoes, all the things my aunt wouldn't have in the house – she said it was criminal to eat out of tins when fresh food was there for the asking . . . or the cooking.

Ten minutes later there was still no sign of Mum, so I sat down same as usual on the settee and switched on the telly. Mum doesn't mind; she always says to do it if I want. There wasn't much on – a 'cowie' of a sort. I watched it without taking it in. I was wondering about whether Mum was going to sleep here or down the town. She'd said she might go down the town with a friend so as I could use her bed. I'd said I didn't mind the settee but she'd seemed set on it – going down the town. So I was sitting there wondering what she'd decided and hoping she'd stay here and put me on the settee, when I heard a bike. It came in the yard, idled a bit and stopped. I got up and knelt on the settee. I could see out the window . . . just. A young bloke I recognized as one I'd seen out here before was propping up his bike. Then I heard the door shoved open and I knew he was coming in. I'd hardly time to turn and sit down straight before this door opened and he walked in, cool as a cucumber.

He looked as surprised to see me as I was him.

'Hey.'

'Hullo.'

'Have you seen Rachel?'

'No,' I said. Somehow it sounded funny hearing him call Mum by her first name. 'I expect she'll be back soon,' I said, kind of prim. That's how he made me. He made me want to pull down my skirt and button up my blouse. It was the way he looked. He whistled under his breath and walked round. It seemed like he'd come to stay.

After a bit he looked my way again.

'Interview?' he asked. 'You come about a job?'

'Oh no,' I said. 'I'm . . . related.'

'Oh I see,' he said. 'Sorry.'

He didn't look sorry, though, he looked amused. He was quite tall with wavy hair and blue eyes, real nice ones; I could have done with them. I couldn't stand him looking at me, half curious, half amused, so I pretended to look at the telly.

'Any good?' He came and sat the other end of the settee.

'All right,' I said. Then, 'Were you expecting to find my mother in?'

'Your *what*?' he said.

I felt myself getting red slowly, neck, cheeks, forehead, till my whole face was burning.

'My mother,' I said.

'You serious?'

'Yes,' I said. 'Why not?'

'How old are you?'

'Close on seventeen.'

'She must'a been fifteen then, when she had you.'

'No—' I began, then it dawned on me Mum probably let people believe she was younger than she was, so I shut up. 'I think she was just out of school,' I said.

'Embarrassed, are you?'

'No,' I said. 'Why?'

'Dunno. That's the impression I got.'

There was a silence, except for the telly, which was into the gunfight. He watched it, intent. I watched because I didn't know what else to do. I'd have liked to have gone out but I thought it would seem rude, so I stayed. He got so wrapped up in it I could look at him without him noticing. He was a real looker, a bit of a Rod Stewart if you like that type. Then the film ended and he got up and switched off.

'You didn't want it, did you?'

'No,' I said. Then, 'Have you come about a job . . . or are you just a friend?' The minute I'd said it I knew how silly it'd sound.

He looked amused. 'Just a friend,' he said.

I could feel myself going red again, so I went on quick hoping he wouldn't notice. 'Do you live out Asherford?' I asked.

'Yep,' he said, nodding.

'So you know my mum quite well?'

'Since I been living out here with her, yes,' he said.

I don't think I ever felt so silly.

Rachel isn't expecting Joe. He has told her he'll be away, that he is going down to Cornwall looking for part-time work. His present job finishes at the end of the week, so she believes him – or sees no reason not to. But Joe has changed his mind. It is as simple as that. Predictability is not one of his strengths, and Cornwall seems an effort he doesn't care to make with Rachel's welcoming bed firmly set in Devon. She is becoming rather a bind, more so now that Diane has turned up. In fact she is becoming tiresomely possessive, for after all she *is* old enough to be his mother and should realize it, Joe reasons. Surely it is obvious he'd prefer a girl his own age? But this particular weekend Diane has inconveniently gone away. In any case, he doesn't know Diane very well . . . yet. Not well enough to spend the night with her. Everything is hampered by her still living at home.

Joe looks across at Tamsin sprawled on the settee. In the

last two hours he has discovered all that Tamsin cares to tell, which, with the free use of Rachel's tucked-away gin, has proved enlightening. To start with Rachel is much older, must be, than she has led him to suppose. Secondly, she's a bad lot; she's abandoned her poor little kiddies, which allows Joe an easier conscience over his two-timing with her and Diane. Thirdly, he finds Tamsin rather appealing. She seems to him like a new model of Rachel – shinier, faster, altogether more zippy. Probably needs oiling . . .

The door suddenly opens. Rachel comes in, quietly and unobtrusively. Tamsin, on her third glass of gin, looks at her bravely. She is smoking, Rachel observes, and as far as she knows Tamsin doesn't smoke. She looks from one to the other. How long have they been together? How much have they . . . discussed? How much of herself is still clothed, unstripped? Rachel lights herself a cigarette and inhales deeply, surely it must calm her, give her time to think? She is aware that they are both speaking but does not hear what they say. Tamsin's legs are crossed above the knee, her skirt seems to have ridden up, she seems . . . different, altered. Worst of all she seems in some indefinable manner aligned with Joe. Rachel feels left out, like a mother. She feels older, her age. She is convinced her skin is wrinkling, especially her neck. She daren't turn her head in case it causes her neck to crease. She wishes she had worn her high-neck black sweater she got at Joan's.

Tamsin is looking at her strangely. Is there something wrong with her appearance? She's speaking.

'I came early – for the weekend.'

Then she has been here a long time, and Joe too, probably.

'Is it all right if I stay?'

Rachel doesn't dare to look at Joe slopped in the chair on her left, she is certain he's laughing at her, behind her back. She spins round to catch him at it but his face is serious and bored. He yawns. What is she to say? Shall she let Tamsin stay? She'll have to. It's late and there's really no way of getting rid of her; unless Joe takes her home on his bike. Rachel shudders at the thought. She sees the full moon in her imagination with Joe and Tamsin silhouetted. She shakes her head trying to get rid of the morbid image. She loves them both after all, in different ways. Well, she must do. Why couldn't Joe have gone to Cornwall like he said? It is all so unreasonable, more than she can be expected to cope with. Tamsin is waiting for an answer.

'Yes, of course you can stay if you want.'

Tamsin looks pleased and relieved. Joe gets up.

'I'll be getting along then.'

Rachel panics.

'There's no need. Tamsin'll sleep in here on the settee.'

Joe smiles at her. Diane passes before his eyes. He'll save himself for Diane, he feels superstitious about it, as though Diane will have him if he denies himself. Is he denying himself Rachel? Well he would have been a month back, and she's still the same person, it's just that she's familiar and . . . old. Joe feels the double-crosser he is, must be.

'I think I'd better go all the same,' he says. 'Ta-ta, Tamsin. See you.' And he makes his way over to the door. Rachel follows.

Outside there is a moon as she has predicted. Isn't Joe even going to kiss her?

'Joe?'

'What is it?' He's bending over the wheel of his Triumph.

'Aren't you even going to say goodnight?'

He squeezes her hand, turns her face up to his. She shudders with the desire that floods her body; she is soft, pliable, all Joe's. He pulls back.

'When?'

He shrugs. 'One day in the week maybe.' The engine roars. Even the moon seems to quiver as the motorbike blasts out of the yard and over the small, humped bridge.

Rachel goes back in the house. Tamsin is sitting on the edge of the settee. She looks ready to run. Rachel looks bitterly at the flushed face and bright dark eyes of her daughter. Of course Joe must have been attracted. He couldn't have failed to be, could he?

'He's ever so nice.'

'Glad you liked him.' Rachel scratches round straightening the two cushions. Tamsin stands up. Silence encloses the mother and daughter in a cell of separateness. Rachel feels she can't breathe. She opens a window.

'I've brought my sleeping bag.' Tamsin is pulling a shiny blue bag from its shiny blue skin. She spreads it over the ochre settee.

'Take this cushion for your head.' Rachel hands her the one she had just plumped up. She feels as though the cushion is Joe; she is handing Joe to Tamsin, relinquishing him: Joe and Tamsin. She feels sick, cold. Her life is over, it must be.

'Thanks.'

Tamsin is undoing the zip of her skirt uncertainly. Rachel knows she wants her to go but decides to stay. She sits down, lights a cigarette and watches Tamsin undress. Tamsin is in her tights tugging at her bra. It comes undone and before she turns away Rachel sees the round apples of her breasts. Could hers have ever been like that? Perfect? It is true Tamsin is a little fat, but smooth, inviting, somehow fresh.

Tamsin is wriggling into her sleeping bag. Rachel stands up.

'Will you be warm enough?'

'It's very warm.'

Tamsin is looking at her imploringly like a spaniel. Rachel forces herself to take a step forward, bend and kiss her on the forehead.

'Goodnight.'

'Goodnight, Mum. Hope I'm not a nuisance.' The brown eyes are looking anxiously up.

'Glad to have you.' Well she would have been if it hadn't been for Joe. She walks to the door and switches up the light switch.

'Sleep well.'

'Yes, and you.'

Rachel's room is damp. The bed looks bleak and lonely. She turns on the radio. It is 'God Save the Queen.'

I didn't sleep all that good. Too much was going round in my head. I kept seeing Joe's face, then Mum's. It took a bit of getting used to the idea of it. It brought me up sharp, made me see things different, made me realize Mum was a person, not just my mother. I quite liked it really, him being young. I thought an old bloke might have been frightening, more like Dad. But all in all, I wished she didn't have anyone. I think I was jealous. I didn't like the idea of her being close with Joe. I wanted her to myself. I hoped Joe'd clear out though I liked him well enough. I thought of the farm once or twice too. Dora and Ron and Dad. It all seemed like another part of my life; past. I didn't ever want to go back – except to get Tom, maybe.

Next time I woke up the sun was shining in and Mum was drawing back the curtains. She was dressed.

'I'm off, then. I've got some things to see to. I'll be back round the dinner hour.'

I tried not to sound disappointed. 'OK,' I said. 'See you then.'

Mum rummaged in her bag, clipped it shut and went out. I heard her high heels clipping off across the yard.

I lay for quite a time looking at two flies gliding round the light-bulb up on the ceiling, then I dressed. I got out the clothes I'd brought special: new skirt, T-shirt, the rest were old. My boots I'd had two years but I'd polished them up. I did my hair careful and put on some eyeliner. Then I took my shoulder bag and went out. I thought I'd go down the town. It wasn't often I was near enough shops to walk.

I knew there was a café in Fore Street so I made for that. Coffee for breakfast instead of tea. I fancied that. I opened my purse, made sure I'd got enough.

When I got there the jukebox was going, there were half a dozen others sat around the tables. They looked at me as I came in. I felt self-conscious as anything but I wasn't going to let them know, so I walked to a table up on the left and sat down. The waitress came and I ordered coffee and a waffle with maple syrup and cream. I was doing myself proud. While I was waiting I glanced at the others, furtive, so as they wouldn't see I was looking. One lot got up and went out. The other couple I guessed were married, sat silent, never speaking, gazing out the window. Three more were my age or a bit older, two boys and a girl. The girl looked pretty hot stuff; she was giggling and carrying on, really amusing the boys, or that's how it seemed. I felt ever so envious. Imagine me sitting at ten a.m. drinking coffee with two blokes. I couldn't.

Then the door-bell tinkled and someone else came in. I wanted to look round but didn't dare, not without them seeing. So I sipped my coffee and waited to see where whoever it was would sit.

The girl with the boys screwed her head round.

'Hey, look who's here.'

'Hi.' They all looked pleased as punch to see whoever it was.

Next minute I saw who it was for myself as he sat down with them. It was Joe. I wished I could fade away, shrink through the floor. He must have thought I looked such a dope sitting on my own. I wished I hadn't put on the eyeliner and my new skirt; he was bound to think I looked silly, all dressed up and nowhere to go. He didn't see me for a bit, he was so busy with them. Then he looked across. He was surprised, I could see that. He nodded. I smiled. He said something to them and came across.

'On your own then?'

'Mum's gone down town, working.'

He hesitated a moment; then, 'Come and join us.'

'I'm not stopping long,' I said. 'Just for a cup of coffee.' At that moment the waitress arrived with my waffle and cream. I could feel him thinking I was greedy. Why had I had to order it?

'Bring it with you,' he said.

'I'll finish up,' I said. 'Then I'll come.'

So I did. I hated every mouthful of that waffle, I only ate half, enough to make the waitress think I hadn't forgotten it. Then I got up and went across. Joe introduced me. Les, Don, and Diane. Diane looked me over. I got the feel I was treading on her territory. They went on with their conversation and I listened, mostly. Except when Joe asked me one or two questions. I didn't feel comfortable but it was better than sitting on my own; except when the waitress came over and asked me if I'd finished and would I pay. They all watched me taking the money out of my purse. I think they thought I was rich, except for Joe. He knew better.

Finally they all got up to go so I went too. In the doorway Joe hung back a bit and asked me what I was doing.

'Nothing,' I said. 'Going down the shops.'

'You can come along to Mike's if you like,' he said. 'It's where I stay when I'm not along at the garage.' He was very casual, confident and all. I could see what my mother saw in him.

'All right,' I said.

So he wandered down the pavement ahead of me, shouldering his way through the screwed-up faces of the shoppers, and I followed wishing I hadn't got so much heel on my boots because it slowed me down. At least I was doing something, I thought. Living.

Tom hangs over the clear water of the pool and sees his own face ripple, crinkle and distort. His face is a nuisance; he's looking for trout. Behind him on the bank is his rod cut from the hedge. Attached to it is a fine piece of line given him by Ron, on the end a hook with a wriggling worm. Beside it stands a jam-jar containing more worms – too big, probably. The one wriggling on his hook is just right. He crawls back carefully from the pool, takes his 'rod' and creeps to a vantage point round the back of an old tree-stump. Carefully he edges nearer and lowers the worm into the water. Almost immediately a tug. Tom lifts his rod; with it comes the line and a small tortured trout, firmly hooked in the gill. Tom lands it, frees it, and bashes its head fiercely on a stone. He lays it in the long grass, chooses another worm, the smallest, and tries again.

The black cat from Ventnor, out hunting for himself, comes to see Tom, finds the fish lying invitingly in the long grass, picks it up and lopes off through the trees. Tom sees him, drops everything, runs, yells. His fish he was going to take home! The black cat leaps up a hedge and drops the fish in fright at Tom's fury. Tom seizes it, nurses it tenderly, thinks a moment, then puts it in his pocket.

Dora sits in the kitchen, her mind on Tamsin. Today is Saturday. Tamsin was away last night, will be away tonight and should be back on Sunday. The truth is Dora misses Tamsin, her surrogate daughter. She says to Ron:

'I dare say the Bawdens'll fill her head with a lot of no-good fancies.'

Ron is having his after-lunch doze. He opens one eye, a habit Dora particularly resents. It seems so lazy, somehow, not to be able to open two eyes. Ben has gone off, no one knows where. He left yesterday evening and the postman hadn't come across him so far this morning. Usually he reports Ben's car parked up on the moor under a hedge.

'I suppose Ben'll be home for his tea.' Dora speaks her thoughts. Ron grunts. Does this mean he agrees or thinks her optimistic? Dora can't seem to relax. It's because she's worried about Tamsin; or so she tells herself. That she is jealous doesn't cross her mind, because Dora imagines she has never known jealousy. Though, thinking back, she wonders, shudders to think, could jealousy be that dreadful darkness she felt when Ben ran after Rachel? No wonder, though, considering the kind of woman Rachel was. And she was quite right, for look what happened. So it wasn't jealousy after all, but just good sound common sense. Disturbingly, she now has exactly that same feeling, so almost certainly a disaster is in store for Tamsin in the same way that it was for Ben.

Dora gets up and tidies the kitchen. Edith is dropping in

later. She hopes Ron will have gone out. She doesn't like Ron or Ben to listen when she has a woman friend, it prevents . . . confidences. She pushes a pin back into her hair as she looks at herself in the mirror over the mantel. Perhaps Edith will have news.

An hour later the front door opens and Edith's voice calls brightly:

'Dora? Are you in?' Of course she is, she is always in. She looks resentfully at Ron; surely there must be something to do outside.

'Edith's here.'

Ron lowers his feet on to the floor. Edith enters, talking, and sits, still talking, on the window seat. Ron puts on his boots but shows no sign of going. Dora looks at him meaningfully. The small talk about damsons, prices down the market, and the parish council's plans for the church roof is running out. If Ron doesn't go soon the news Edith has obviously called to bring must go unspoken.

'I thought you said to remind you to do that gate,' Dora says pointedly.

Ron grunts, he feels sleepy still and secretly rather enjoys Edith's gossip. It is a small weakness in an otherwise restrained man – and never goes any further, he consoles himself. Outside it is raining mistily and the wind is battering the panes; there is nothing he feels less like than doing that gate. Dora divines his train of thought.

'Or if not the gate, then the clutch on the tractor.'

Edith joins with her. 'Poor Ron – there's always something to be done on a farm. I said to Arthur before he retired, "Arthur," I said, "you can be thankful you've only got the one kidney – it's as good a reason as any for giving up your own place. You'd do better to sell up and give a hand out Barnett's." He agrees with me now though he didn't at the time, I'm sure.'

Ron is sure too. Poor Arthur, who'd want to be him with nothing to do but sit in a bungalow listening to Edith and helping out others? – the fate of most local farmers no

44

longer fit enough to manage on their own. Their wives like the change; no draughts and dirty corners and more chance to get down the village for company. Who wants to end their days on the lonely moor? Certainly not the women.

Rod drags himself slowly to his feet, rubs his back and straightens it. Tom comes in, sees Edith and makes for the scullery.

'Caught one, then?' Ron brings him up short. Tom slides his fish from his pocket. Dora is incensed.

'How many times have I told you *not* to put a fish in your jacket pockets?'

But Tom is not listening. He and Ron are examining the fish. They put it on the scales: nearly three quarters of a pound. Tom is delighted. He slithers like the fish past Dora and out the back to gut it. Ron too goes out. At last! Dora heaves a sigh of relief. Now perhaps she will hear why Edith has come.

Rachel gets back to the garage at one o'clock sharp. Tamsin isn't there waiting as she expected. She goes over to the other part of the garage where Alf is respraying a wing. No, he hasn't seen her. Rachel feels annoyed. After all, she's made excuses and hurried back all for nothing. She goes into her kitchen and opens tins of beans and sardines for herself, makes herself a toasted sandwich. She thought they might do something this afternoon but now look. What's the point? She switches on the immersion heater and waits for it to heat up. She may as well have a bath. Her part-time venture as an agent for cosmetics hasn't gone too well. She lies on the settee with a cold flannel on her forehead. Doubtless she will be laid off. Is it true they are keeping only three out of five? And if so, why does she have to be one of the two to go? They have murmured about her having other employment in the garage, but she's told them it doesn't amount to anything. Certainly it doesn't enable her to keep Joe in the manner he prefers, and how else is she to keep him? Her head jerks involuntarily; it is her nerves. She takes two pills, then remembers Tamsin.

Wretched girl! Where has she got to? Her mind moves to Joe. Where is he? Surely he must want to see Tamsin if not herself? An unpleasant thought crosses her mind for a few seconds, long enough to agitate, to disrupt. Can it be that Joe and Tamsin are together? Rachel gets up and tests the water. Still not hot. She paces about in agitation and looks out of the window. Oh God, why is all her life such torture? She has a go at the hidden gin, observes it has gone down. Surely that and the pills will do it? They do. She begins to feel light-headed, a little dizzy. She hums. Yes, the water is hot. She runs a steaming bath and climbs in, lies back. Nothing seems to matter any more. The water is gentle, womb-like. She almost falls asleep. Then the front door opens.

'Who's there?'

Footsteps.

'It's only me.' Tamsin's head looks in at her.

'Where have you been? I've had my lunch.'

'I went down the town.'

'All the shops shut between one and two.'

'Yes. I'm very sorry. Actually I met Joe.'

Rachel stiffens. All her senses come back to her on the instant. She feels herself made up of live wires.

'Joe?'

'Yes. He showed me his garage, where he keeps his bike.'

And what else did he show you? Rachel wonders. She feels cold all over in spite of the steam: her worst fear come true. She has known all along, from the first moment she saw them together.

'I thought we might have gone out but now it's too late.'

'I'm terribly sorry.' Tamsin sounds near to tears; serve her right. Rachel feels at a disadvantage in the bath. She erupts from the water with a swirl and grasps the green towel from the rail.

'I'll be with you in a moment.'

Tamsin edges out backwards, closing the door. Rachel towels herself violently. Should she send Tamsin packing,

46

tell her it's not convenient, anything? Make something up? She turns to the mirror and bares her teeth, taking up the toothbrush. The toothbrush's motion restores proportion. She is, after all, Tamsin's mother and has no *evidence* that anything is going on. No, she mustn't do anything precipitate, it would be shaming, humiliating. They might both guess her reason. She must rather conceal her suspicions, act normally. Rachel creams her face into the youngest and most tranquil expression it can muster, takes her bathrobe from the hook on the back of the door and goes out to Tamsin.

'So you see?' Dora is sitting on one end of the window seat opposite Edith on the other, both of them hold cups and saucers.

Edith looks puzzled. 'But are you sure?'

'I know she went about a job, that I do know. I heard from Hilda who's working down the Asherford Co-op.'

'If she's got work out the garage what would she be going about this other job for?' Edith's cup wobbles dangerously as she lifts it to her lips. Sometimes Dora's convolutions of thought are hard to follow.

'Exactly.' Dora is triumphant. 'She must be losing the job out the garage – it stands to reason.'

Edith looks unconvinced. 'She may be just after extra. Besides—' 'She breaks off tantalizingly.

Dora waits.

'Besides . . .' She pauses. 'She's got a young fellow living in along of her.'

The momentous piece of information is out at last, carefully contained and nursed by Edith till just the right moment for its maximum effect. Edith has an inborn sense of drama.

Dora puts down her cup. 'In the back of the garage?'

'He comes and goes.' Edith adds a sense of mystery.

Dora settles her cup safely on the corner of the stove.

'You mean she's . . . keeping him?'

'That's not what I said. But I mean to say, he's a lot

47

younger. Laid off now they say, so I shouldn't wonder if Rachel isn't supporting him.'

Dora stares at Edith a few seconds, taking in the full import of what she has just heard.

'She ought to be ashamed of herself,' she pronounces.

'He gets his dole money, I suppose.' Edith, seeing that she has worked Dora to a pitch, becomes placatory.

Dora sniffs, wipes her nose. 'It isn't going to do the Bands any good having her down there making a fool of herself, is it? I just hope Tamsin doesn't get to hear of it.'

Dora stands up and refills the pot.

'Bound to, I should have thought.' Edith prides herself on her foresight; sometimes she believes herself something of a seer. She accepts a refill to her cup. Several 'strangers', she notes, float on the surface. She says nothing to Dora, who regards Edith's superstitions as anti-chapel, even black magic. Dora doesn't hold with it. But at the present Dora's mind is elsewhere.

'Do you know if the Bawdens are still in Asherford?'

'If they have moved it must be recent.' Edith doesn't like to be caught uncertain. She coughs, drinks her tea and takes her cup to the sink.

'You're not going?' Dora's tone is tragic.

'I must.' Edith looks round for her bag. 'If I hear any more,' she says, spying her bag beside the table leg, 'I'll certainly tell you.'

Dora has no doubt of this but she would still like to prolong Edith's visit. The rest of the weekend stretches ahead of her without Tamsin. Tamsin listens to her. Tamsin is another woman in a predominantly male environment. The men inhabit a different landscape to Dora, theirs is exterior, made up of facts, Dora thinks. Hers is interior, made up of details and feelings, of colours, curtains, recipes, chapel, and talk; above all, talk, human intercourse. Dora sighs for her own loneliness in the midst of her matriarchy. What will she do when Tamsin leaves home for good? There is still Tom, but recently Tom has started to ignore her like his uncles. He listens to her with patience, answering when necessary, but he almost never speaks to her, never divulges his thoughts.

Edith is talking and Dora has actually not heard. Edith looks at her curiously.

'Don't take it hard, dear. Whatever Rachel is about won't reflect on you and yours. You made that plain to everyone when she up and left her kiddies all those years back. Don't you worry.'

'But I do.' Dora's control slips dangerously. 'I worry for Tamsin. What if Rachel gets hold of her, takes her in? You know the way she has with some.'

Edith has seldom seen Dora so . . . revealed. She feels uncomfortable and inadequate. What is it exactly that Dora is trying to tell her? She edges towards the door and is saved from the emotional scene she dreads by the arrival of Tom, who goes round the kitchen opening drawers, stirring up their contents and half-closing them again with oddments left hanging out like tongues.

'What are you looking for?' Dora's voice has resumed its normal sharp tone.

'A ruler. I want to measure my fish.'

'Shut the drawers proper. There's one in the desk in my office.'

Tom barges out with a happy oblivion of all but his own needs, but as he goes he hears his aunt say:

'You don't think Tamsin's with her, then?' And Edith answers: 'I wouldn't like to say for sure, but you've taught her what's what, you've done your bit, and now it's up to her.'

Tom wonders what exactly is up to Tamsin, but a moment later forgets as he sees the desired ruler in the corner of the large, neat desk. He seizes it and returns to the scullery where his silvery-brown and spotted fish lies glistening on the wooden drainer.

Ben opens his eyes and sees a strange landscape. He blinks, then remembers. He is somewhere on the moor. He sits up a bit more. His foot has cramp. He grasps it and pulls up the

toe. The cramp is alleviated. Ben again observes his surroundings but they mean nothing to him. How has he got
where he is, wherever that is? There is not much of the
moor he doesn't know, but this bit, darn him if he knows
where he's got to. The car is at an angle and the skyline
slopes correspondingly, hills with a few thorn and a stone
wall tracking up. He opens the door and climbs out. He
walks down the hedge and relieves himself. As he fastens
his zip he hears a car approaching. He ducks down, unwilling to face questions of even a sympathetic nature. The car
passes. He looks after it and notices it contains a young
couple; it's going slowly as though also looking for a place
to park. Ben shakes his head; he's not feeling good. He
clambers into the front seat, buries his face in his arms on
the steering wheel and waits for sleep.

Surprisingly and upsettingly, sleep does not come.
Instead thoughts fill Ben's head, thoughts that Ben has not
asked for, has certainly not invited to dance before his
closed eyes in a series of lurid pictures. He rubs his eyes,
shakes his head. It makes no difference. Rachel is there,
walking through Meridan in high heels swinging a basket.
What does she think she's doing? Doesn't she know everyone's looking at her in the wrong way, laughing at her?
She's making a fool of herself, and Ben too. He hurries up
behind her, grabs her. She swings the basket in his face.
The picture flames red. He seizes her wrists. Shouts come
from all sides. He takes no notice, only forces her wrists
down, crosses them. Her laughing mouth is wide, full of
pain, agony. The picture cuts off sharp. Rachel is holding
Tamsin, sitting up in bed. 'Open the window, Ben! Go on,
open it.' But he's nervous of opening it; it may kill her so
soon after giving birth. 'Open it.' He opens it; he doesn't
want to displease her, upset her just now with a new-born
baby girl: his child. He pushes open the window. The birds
are singing . . . sun . . . snow melting in the yard. He treads
carefully back across the floorboards to the bed, looks
down on the baby. 'Pull the strap off my shoulder, Ben.' He
does so, stares amazed at the blue-veined swollen breast. Is

that Rachel's? She pushes her tit into the baby's mouth; it cries, refuses to take it. He stands there, useless. 'Shall I hold its head?' 'No, go away.' He is dismissed. He blunders downstairs, his heart full of an agony, a guilt he can't explain. There she is again, in front of him swinging a basket. He'll kill her this time. Why isn't she home with the baby? She turns as he comes up close. It's Tamsin's eyes looking at him, Tamsin's face. Like she looked yesterday when she came in from school, asked to spend the night away. The picture goes black; black and green circles loom at Ben behind his closed eyes. There is a roaring in his head too. A large cattle-truck rumbles past along the road. Ben is asleep.

'He's coming along later,' I said. 'About four.'

'What for?' Mum's tone was sharp. She sat opposite me in the chair, her one knee crossed over the other, her bathrobe fallen away. She lit herself a fag. I thought she'd kill herself of lung cancer but didn't like to say. She didn't offer me one.

'He just said he'd drop round.' Mum didn't look pleased. I wondered what was up. I got the feeling it was something I'd done but I couldn't think what – unless she minded me talking to Joe, which didn't seem likely. True enough we'd spent the morning together, but with a friend of his in a shed with pieces of bike. Mostly I'd hung about while they'd pulled apart an engine. I'd told Mum this and she'd said: 'You don't have to account for how you spend your time. I'm not your keeper.' It had knocked me back. I suppose I hadn't seen the difficult side of her up until then and I had missed dinner by having it with them. We'd gone in his friend's house and helped ourselves from his fridge, drunk some brown ale too. Then I'd taken myself off, but I'd gone down the wrong street and been longer than I thought.

'Did you get a lot of new samples?' I asked. I knew what she'd been about.

She seemed to brighten up a bit then. She picked up the

briefcase stood on the floor and opened it on her lap. I moved over and sat on the arm of the chair beside her. It looked like the best Christmas present you could get: samples of lipstick all different shades, tinted moisturizers, eye-shadow, pencils, creams, the lot. I drew my breath in when I saw it.

'Wish I could try 'em,' I said.

'Well, you can't,' said Mum, but not hastily. She picked out one and took a look at it, tried it on the back of her hand, then handed it to me.

'Go on. Try it.'

Mum's like that – unpredictable. Says one thing and does another and changes from one mood to another in an instant. It's as though it's an effort for her to be cross, she gets fed up and snaps out of it. That's how it was then. All at once everything was all right.

I took it over to the mirror and coloured my lips very careful round the edges, then filled in the centre. Mum came over and stood behind watching me, then she handed me an eye-shade. While I was applying it, she went and rummaged about in a cupboard in her bedroom and came back with a hat. It was straw, covered in cherries and spotted net, really chic.

'Mum,' I said. 'Wherever did you get it?'

'Jumble,' she said. 'Bit of luck, wasn't it?'

She placed it carefully on my head.

'Line your eyes with brown,' she said. I did. Then I stood up straight and both of us looked at me.

'You look good enough to marry a lord,' she said.

'Do I?' I said pleased.

Then she took it off me and put it on herself. We both looked at her.

'Suits you,' I said.

She pulled it off. 'It's better on you.' She put it back on my head. 'Keep it, if you like.'

'When'd I wear it?'

'Any time,' she said. 'Wear it to chapel on Sunday and give 'em all a shock.'

I giggled. 'I can't imagine Auntie letting me,' I said.

'You're grown now,' my mother said firm. 'You do what you please, not what your aunt tells you, else you'll spend all your days minding pigs.'

'It's difficult, though,' I said, 'when I'm living at home.'

'Move out, then,' she said. 'Make yourself independent.'

'I got to finish school first,' I said, disconcerted.

She shrugged. She seemed indifferent. I felt hurt. I'd set store by my learning. I'd thought she had too.

'Don't you think it matters,' I asked, 'finishing school?'

It's up to you.' She reached up and took the hat off my head.

'I'll put it away for now, anyways.' She put it back in her cupboard because I heard the doors.

'When did you say he was coming?' she called through.

I thought for a moment. 'Four,' I said.

She came back through with a roll of cotton-wool in her hand.

'It's nearly four now,' she said. 'Go in the bathroom and clean up your face.'

I took the roll and did as she said. I hated to do it. I really liked my new face but I didn't care to cross her – not now she was all right again.

When I went back Mum was sitting in her chair with the briefcase closed up on her lap.

'Thing is Tamsin,' she said, 'I got to have more money. I'm owing.'

'Owing?' I said, surprised. I'd thought she was earning good pay.

She sighed. 'They're laying me off. Well they haven't said, but I'm pretty certain.'

She said it quite simple but I could feel for her it was serious. I wanted to help, say something, but what could I do?

'Can't you get anything else part time?' I suggested.

'Not very likely,' she said, 'with the unemployment figures as they are.'

She was silent for a bit, then she said:

53

'Joe takes a bit of keeping, see.'

I stared at her. 'Doesn't he earn for himself?'

'Not now,' she said. 'Not since the motorway work closed down for winter. He picks up a bit on social security but nothing to speak of.'

I was quiet for a bit, taking in my mother was keeping Joe. It came as a shock, but it wasn't the only shock that morning. The next came harder.

'I borrowed £50 out of the cash till. I've got to get it back by Friday because my boss is coming over to check it out. Can you get me any, Tamsin?'

'I don't have £5, let alone £50,' I said.

'I know,' she said, 'but Dora keeps a bit put by out at the farm, doesn't she? She always used to keep the milk money till the end of the month.'

I felt a bit dizzy. What was Mum suggesting? That I go and nick a bit out of the farm cash-box?

'I can't, Mum,' I said, 'if that's what you meant.'

'Only to borrow,' she said. 'I'll pay you back the same evening, after he pays me. My boss. It's just the register's got to come out right, see?'

I saw.

She had got up and was looking out the window.

'Anyway, think about it,' she said. 'Joe's here now.' I heard the noise of his engine pull up outside. I didn't know whether I was coming or going. Nothing looked the same as it had half an hour back. One thing was plain: she didn't want it discussed in front of Joe.

Dora and Ron face each other across the table. Tom sits on the third side; the fourth remains empty. Ben is still 'missing'. The postman has scoured his comprehensive routes but found, if not nothing, certainly not Ben. He is puzzled. So are they all. Dora panics. Supposing he is dead, has turned his car over? Is trapped inside or has long since been consumed by fire and is now watching her from Heaven? She hopes it is Heaven.

Looking across the table at Ron her face hardens.

'Shouldn't you go out looking for him?' she asks for the twentieth time that day.

Ron ignores the question; he gives no indication he has heard.

'It's easy for you, Ron Band, to sit there complacent, but I mean to say he is your own brother.'

Ron adjusts his glasses and considers the silliness of his sister. He has always thought her stupid; the frequency with which she repeats the former question confirms his prior knowledge. Does she really imagine he will find Ben just like that? Ben knows the moor like the back of his hairy hand – the furze and rocks, lanes and laybys. Ron has to give him that. Ben knows the moor, better than he does; but then Ben spends his life up there one way or the other, while Ron spends his on Ventnor. There isn't a stone, a boulder or a tree in a bank on Ventnor Ron doesn't know. Nor a dip in the field, nor the places where the springs'll come up in wet weather. Yes, he knows his farm. He sighs; he tenses himself against the next onslaught from Dora. Tom, he notices, has disappeared. Where? Out? Not on a night like this – it's too rough. As if to confirm this the wind booms in a violent gust down the big open chimney. The ragged curtain concealing most of the hearth flaps and billows like a spinaker.

'Think I'll go up,' he says, standing.

'You mean you won't go looking?' Dora asks once more, resentment lacing her restrained voice.

'Won't see nothing tonight,' Ron says with satisfaction.

'No, but if you'd gone when I first asked it might'a been different. Ben might be sitting here at this table, same as usual.'

Ron unaccountably remembers a ghost he's read about somewhere. He feels uneasy. Not that he's superstitious because he isn't, it's just some things . . . He walks to the stair door and tugs it open.

'Tamsin'll be back tomorrow, I suppose,' he says.

There is no reply. Dora is blowing her nose. Ron hurriedly closes the door and goes up the stairs. He notices Tom has a light on in his room as he passes.

Tom is sitting over the table in the corner of his many-cornered room bending over a map of the moor. His right hand is raised and from it dangles a small metal bead on the end of a thread. It waves vaguely round and back and forth. Tom glances intently from it to the map, and then back again. He lowers it a fraction. Yes, it is definitely changing its motion, revolving. Ben must be there. He places his finger on the point on the map and draws the lamp nearer. Kember, right down on the South Moor. Tom's heart beats with excitement. He'll go there tomorrow and look. How? He doesn't know but he'll find a way. And if his pendant works for Ben, what else may it not work for? Tom sees himself standing with a group of police and their dogs, giving them instructions, pointing the way.

He takes off his trousers and gets into bed in the rest of his clothes – too cold to take off more. Though the walls of Ventnor are thick the wind seems to blow right through when it's from the east. Tom lies gazing at the square of paler sky through the window light. His future has never looked so simple and rosy as it does on this particular evening of his life.

Rachel, Joe and Tamsin sit together watching the telly. Joe sits one end of the settee, his long legs sprawled, his arms up with his hands behind his head. Tamsin sits the other, neatly, pressed as far away from Joe as possible. There is a cushion between them because fortunately it is a three-seater. Rachel sits in her chair, from which she can see the telly and the settee equally well.

Joe seems to be enjoying the sit. com. for every now and then he lets out a roar of laughter and changes his position. Tamsin giggles from time to time to show she is not without humour and because she feels it is expected of her. In fact she doesn't find it at all funny and hates almost all sit. coms.

Rachel has not the faintest idea what is taking place on the screen. She is thinking how they will all spend the night, and also about the money for the till. Straightening things out suddenly seems quite possible now she has had the idea of borrowing a bit from the farm. Why, after all, shouldn't the farm do something for her? Even after ten years she is still Ben's wife; she is certainly no one else's. She chews her fingers. She would not be stupid enough to make that mistake twice, no thank you. She glances across at the settee. In the semi-darkness (because the picture is better in the dark) Tamsin looks rather lumpish. Perhaps Joe is not attracted to her. Rachel feels uncertain. It would be much easier if she knew. What a mess, she thinks; who would have thought she, Joe and Tamsin would all be stuck in here for the evening watching telly? But what else is there they can do except spend money they haven't got in the pubs?

The programme ends. Tamsin stretches her legs in relief and sits up. Joe reaches a hand down and plugs in the standard lamp. Rachel gets up, smoothing her skirt. Who would like coffee? They all would. She goes through to the kitchenette.

Tamsin and Joe sit speechless. There is really nothing to say. They would like to be close, touching each other, exploring each other's bodies. A current passes between them despite the cushion dividing them. Speech would spoil this silent communication which is deliciously exciting, the more so for neither one being aware that the other is feeling it.

Rachel in the kitchen wonders about their muteness. She takes it to mean they don't hit it off, have nothing in common, which of course is true. What, she wonders, does *she* have in common with Joe? Probably not much, but then there is the difference in age. Why does she have to keep harping on this? It didn't make any difference at first, so why now? She pours the boiling water on the instant Co-op coffee and chicory and sets the cups on the tray. When she enters the other room, pushing the door with her shoulder,

Tamsin is looking at a magazine and Joe is lying on the settee with his eyes shut.

The silence seems catching. They sit listening to each other's gulps as the hot liquid slides down their throats. Finally Rachel says: 'You must be tired, aren't you Tamsin?'

Tamsin stares at her. 'Not really,' she says.

She's certainly gauche, Rachel thinks. She's at that gauche age. Or is she just putting it on? Surely she realizes that she and Joe are waiting to go to bed together.

Joe drinks the last of his coffee and stands up. 'I must go,' he says, clapping his pockets.

'Go?' Rachel's voice echoes the painful cry of a desolate marshbird to anyone who has a keen ear.

'Get back,' says Joe. 'Don's staying up for me.'

Rachel stands; so does Tamsin. At the door, Joe hesitates and looks back at Tamsin.

'I'll pick you up about three tomorrow, then?'

'If you're sure its not a trouble.'

'No. I want to give the bike a spin anyways.' Joe goes out. Rachel changes her mind. She doesn't follow him. Instead she finds the gin and pours herself the last of it. She drinks, as she and Tamsin listen to the engine fading in the distance.

'Where are you going tomorrow?' Her voice sounds strange, a bit thick.

'Joe's taking me home because there isn't a bus on a Sunday.'

Rachel draws her arm across her forehead. Perhaps she's imagining it all, perhaps there's nothing between them. She must try to stop getting worked up about nothing. If only she could be sure. Automatically she collects the empty cups. Tamsin takes the tray and carries it out, washes up. Rachel stands half behind her with the drying-up cloth. Tamsin doesn't *look* as though she's concealing things, but do people ever? And how can she blame Tamsin, her own daughter, for being exactly like herself? Tamsin finishes, dries her hands, then impulsively puts her

58

arms round her mother and kisses her. Rachel is startled. She returns the kisses while wondering about the motive. Can it be compensating for guilt feelings, or is it spontaneous affection? Alas, it is both, so devious and complex are ways of response. Tamsin herself has no idea why she should suddenly have felt the need to kiss her mother. She imagines it to be natural.

Ben wakes again much later. A watery sun is shining greyly through the windscreen; misty rain drifts past the windows forming a rainbow that fades as soon as he sees it. His head feels heavy and his throat dry. What he needs is a drink, a pint. He pushes himself back in the seat, pulls out the choke and turns the starter key. The engine obliges. Ben puts it into gear and lets off the hand-brake. Five futile minutes of revving and wheel-spinning convince him the car is not to be shifted from the shallow ditch into which he drove it the previous night. He switches off and sits cursing, then struggles out of the now crazily tilted door. His efforts to move the car have merely succeeded in getting the back end wedged on a rock. He walks round, lifts it and shoves, to no effect. If he had someone else to drive he'd be away. He looks all round, still puzzled that he does not recognize any landmark, then starts for the road. He trudges along, head bent into the rain. On one side is a beech hedge, twisted and stunted by the wind; on the other the open moor. A group of ponies sheltering ahead of him hardly bother to shift as he passes; sheep lie in the road or graze the banks. Ben eyes the ponies for a brand that will indicate to him their owner and so his whereabouts, but they are ear-tagged in modern fashion and the tags have grown into the ponies' shaggy winter ears. He continues. Sooner or later where there's a hedge there's a farm, or so Ben believes. Sooner, he hopes. He's never been one for walking. Then unexpectedly tucked in a quarry on his right, he sees a car. He stops, takes it in, and then without any hesitation advances. He tries to look in through the windows, but they are steamed up. Undeterred at the thought of waking the possibly sleeping occupants, Ben bangs on the car door with his fists. At first no sound. Ben repeats his rap. The car rocks, the occupants are shifting. Ben moves a few feet away discreetly and waits. After a few minutes the front door opens. Joe's face emerges, the expression guilty and defensive. When he sees it is only Ben and not the constable he feared, his expression relaxes. Ben advances. Joe takes him to be the farmer owning the quarry where he has parked.

'All right,' he says. 'I only stopped for a rest. I'm going right on.' He's about to shut the door when Ben grasps it.

'I got my ole car stugged on a rock a couple'a hundred yards back up the road. I need a driver.'

Joe's face falls.

'My sister's in the back not feeling too good. I oughter get her home.'

Ben grins. He implies he knows just what's been going on in the back of Joe's car. He probably does.

'We don't need to trouble the lady,' he says. 'If you could just steer while I push, I'll be away.'

Joe agrees. He has little alternative but to do so. What's more Ben assumes a lift.

I thought Dad had come to look for me. I thought it was all up. I was laid there in the back waiting for it. Then when he started on about the car being stuck it began to dawn on me he didn't know I was in there. I didn't waste time, snake-like was the word for how I got on that floor. I just slithered – not a move, not a sound. I knew he couldn't have seen anything through the windows. If there'd been a rug or something, I could have stayed still and covered myself over. As it was there was nothing.

When Dad got in I thought he'd feel me. I felt him all right through the seat cushion. He was half-squashing me. As we drove back up the road I tried to guess what he was doing so far out. We were right down on the edge of the South Moor and Dad doesn't often get off the North, not to my knowledge. He must have had too much and spent the night under the hedge; that wasn't a hard one to spot. I heard him ask Joe where he was and start spinning a yarn how he'd got himself stuck. I could tell Joe didn't believe him. I wondered why Dad bothered.

Then Joe bumped over some rough and stopped. He and Dad got out and I heard them move off. Ever so slow I raised my head and breathed on the window. When a patch cleared I looked out. Joe was sat in the car with the door open and Dad was rocking it. They were having a job, I could see. Any moment I thought Joe would come and get me to help push. He didn't even know I was hiding. He'd never looked back nor nothing. It's true he hadn't spoken, so perhaps he had cottoned on. But I couldn't know for sure, so I sat there looking when I dared, praying he wouldn't come back with Dad and open up the back door.

Then Joe started it up and mud was flying and Dad was heaving. There was a kind of grating noise as it came free of the rock, then it skidded forward, its front half gripping and the back end sliding sideways down the ditch. Dad was scarlet in the face. I wondered if he would burst a blood vessel or his heart or something. But he got the car up and Joe drove it swinging about all over the place out on to the road. He drew up what sounded really close. I couldn't see any more, because I was down behind the seat again. I could hear their voices but not what they said. A door banged, the engine was chugging over, then after what seemed ages it started off, passed us, and drove away. Still I didn't dare move for fear Joe'd gone off in it and Dad was standing outside waiting to get me. It wasn't till Joe put his head over the back seat and tugged my hair I dared even look up.

'Hey' he said. 'You don't need to be that scared. It was only some old bum got his car stugged.'

I sat up slowly. I was so cramped it took a few moments before I could get my leg out straight. The funny thing was I kept opening my mouth to tell Joe it was my father, yet somehow it never got said. I don't think I wanted to be the daughter of some 'old bum' and I really resented Joe for having called him that. So I said nothing and Joe thought me a scarey-nut.

'Once you saw it wasn't the police you didn't need to fuss so much,' he said. 'They can stir up trouble but I never known an ordinary person do more'n kick you out. Still, it's better you kept out of sight because then no gossip'll get round.'

I supposed he meant back to Mum. That we should park near my dad way off his usual beat seemed a chance in a million but it had happened. I still couldn't bring myself to tell Joe. Instead I said:

'I ought to get back soon. They'll be wondering where I'm to.'

'Get in the front then,' he said, and I clambered over beside him. He bent across and kissed me. I couldn't resist it no more than earlier on. I held my mouth up for more; and more. Finally it was him who eased off and turned the starting key.

'Best get you back,' he said.

I let my head lie back against the seat as he drove. I looked at his profile sometimes and at bits of trees as they flashed past the windows. Nothing seemed quite real – too much had happened. I didn't want to think because I dreaded my own thoughts. I didn't want to have to look at what I'd done. I hadn't meant to, hadn't planned anything. It had just happened. That's what I told myself. But was it true? Hadn't something in me known I should never have accepted a lift home from Joe? Then him turning up in a borrowed car. That had knocked my mother back a bit. She hadn't said anything but I could feel.

It was dark outside the car now; Joe's face was dark. He reached his hand on to my thigh. I put my hand over his. But my thoughts were getting a hold on me now. How could I have done it? The meanest thing anyone can do to another she cares for, and I was her daughter. I was pulled in two. The nicest thing that had ever happened to me was the worst thing I'd ever done.

'Joe,' I said, 'I'm rotten, aren't I?'

'What are you on about?' he asked.

'You're my mum's, aren't you?' I said.

'So what?' he said. 'I'm no more hers'n yours.'

I thought about her keeping him but I didn't like to say. Instead I started to worry about the money. I'd promised to try to borrow her some, and now it seemed the least I could do. I fell to planning it and wondering how and when I could get to Auntie's desk without her being around. I thought it'd be impossible except maybe Wednesday, when she went down the market.

'Isn't Ventnor down there?' Joe's voice came out of the dark.

I sat up scared again. He mustn't drive me in; Dad'd see the car.

'The lane's fifty yards along on the left,' I said. 'How did you know?'

'I came out with a friend one Sunday.' He wasn't going to let on any more. I wondered then if it was my mother.

'Let me out at the turning,' I said. 'I'll walk the rest.'

He didn't argue but stopped where I said. I felt for the door handle.

'Here,' he said. He bent across and we kissed again and all the want of him came flooding back. I forced myself away because I imagined Ron behind the wall in the sheep's field, though it wasn't likely; but enough unlikely things had happened that day.

'Bye, Joe,' I said.

'See you,' he said.

Then I was out in the chill clinging mist, and Joe had pulled on, using only his sidelights and no revs, and disappeared round the bend ahead. I listened to the engine winding along the lane into the distance. I wondered if he'd go back to my mother that night.

It wasn't properly dark yet. I stood still till my eyes got used to the dark and then set off down the lane. At the bridge at the bottom I looked over at the black curling water. If I wasn't a coward, I thought, I'd get rid of myself like people did, right then. But I liked living and I was a coward. One thing I didn't like was myself. I despised myself. I knew if I was someone else seeing what I'd done I'd hate myself. I was so ashamed of it I thought I'd never tell anyone. I'd keep it secret till I died.

I walked up the last bit into the yard. On the left an old car shone as a bit of moon came through and caught it. On the right were the buildings. A moo came from the sheds: the calves! I wondered if Tom'd fed them. Outside the back door I could see the shape of Dad's car. I seemed to have had the luck of the devil. If Dad had found me in with Joe . . . I put the thought out my head, it made me feel sick. I reached the porch door and shoved it open. It scraped and jolted across the uneven flags. I could see a light under the kitchen door. I opened it. Auntie was sitting at the table, Ron was by the stove. It was so usual, so familiar, it made all that had happened seem a dream.

'I'm back,' I said, obvious as could be.

'You're late,' said my aunt, predictably.

'Sorry. I had a job getting back up,' I said. We always talked about the moor as 'up' and anywhere off of it as 'down'.

My aunt said nothing but looked as though she would have liked to. Ron shifted his feet.

'Is Dad upstairs?' I asked, my heart in my mouth in case they said he'd seen me or something. He *could* have seen me and said nothing, I thought, but in my heart I didn't believe it. If he'd seen me he'd have yanked me out and hollered at me loud enough to wake every ghost for miles.

'He's out,' Ron said. My heart did miss a beat then. He might have seen me getting out of Joe's car.

'Out where?'

'Getting a breath of fresh air,' said Ron, folding his arms and sitting down again. That was his usual expression to say that Dad had got a hangover. I said nothing but I felt uncomfortable, insecure at the thought of him out wandering. I'd thought he'd be in bed, that's where he usually went after a night out.

'He weren't pleased to find you still out.' My aunt couldn't let it go.

'I think I'll go up,' I said. I helped myself to bread and cheese and Branston pickle. 'Goodnight,' I said, and as I did so a picture of Auntie's desk flashed across my eyes. I blotted it out by opening the stair door and going up.

I sat at my table finishing an essay I had to do for the next day. I couldn't concentrate. I knew it wasn't much good, but what could I do? Eventually I gave up and went back over Joe and me together again and again.

Much later I heard Tom come up. He shook my door.

'Shall I come in?' he said.

'No,' I shouted.

So he went on to his room. I felt mean but I didn't want to speak to anyone. Lying alone on my bed watching the tip of a pine-tree dip and sway against the sky, I decided I loved Joe. That's how it seemed.

Tom is up in the hedge cutting a forked hazel when Ben's car splutters and pops down the lane. Tom thinks he can water-divine as well as locate the whereabouts of his father with a pendulum. He jumps down off the hedge and follows the car into the yard. If his father has been at Kember or even near, then Tom's divining career stretches ahead of him like a straight and friendly road.

Ben gets out, sees Tom but ignores him and goes in the house. Tom follows him at a distance. He's wary of his father during his 'bouts' from past experience, but his need to find out whether Kember is right gives him courage.

Dora, who's cooking rabbits shot by Ron, opens the ring and puts the kettle over. She and Ben acknowledge each other by their silence. Ben sits. Tom hovers.

Finally Dora speaks what is on her mind and also the thing most calculated to upset Ben.

'Your girl's still out.' Dora has that custom of referring to the children as Ben's when they most displease her and are in trouble. By this method she both absolves herself from responsibility and attacks Ben with one blow. Ben, as she has surmised, is not too far gone to rise. He sits up, sits forward on the chair.

'Didn't her come on the mid-day bus?'

'No Ben, she didn't.' Dora pronounces her words carefully as if it will emphasize the situation.

Tom perches himself on the bench and kicks the table leg. He wants to get a word in. Dora chops the swede up with deft, vigorous blows of her knife and heaps it on top of the rabbit in the casserole. She puts on the lid and advances on the oven.

'It was you let her go,' Ben retaliates weakly. Words are not his forte. He takes off his hat and rubs his head. A fury is growing deep down inside him. Tamsin is the only thing left in Ben's uncertain life that can arouse strong feelings; indeed they are so strong that Ben sways before them as a quick-grown tree in front of a violent gust of wind. He is not sure just how far he'll go before his roots will lift.

'Have you rung down Bawdens?'

'No I haven't. I got better things to do than concern myself over a girl who can't bring herself home when she should.' Dora does not pause to wonder about the accuracy of this statement, but it achieves the desired effect. Ben stands unsteadily, makes for the door. Dora knows he is going to the call-box. She waits till he is at the door then asks a question she knows the answer to.

'Have you got any money?'

Ben hasn't. He never has after he has been on a bout; it has been poured away as surely as the beer. The waste infuriates Dora, who takes it out on the humbled Ben. She goes through to the office and takes money from the desk drawer, not the cash-box. She also writes the Bawdens' number clearly on a piece of paper and hands it and 20p to Ben.

'Go on then,' she commands. She has got the upper hand.

Ben goes. But Dora's will is vanquished when, soon after the bridge, Ben stumbles off the road and falls into long grass up against the bank. The rustle of the wind in the holly above him and the damp mist on his face combine to soothe him. His head ached when walking and the road undulated strangely. Here things are better. His head drops on his chest and he slowly slides sideways. At some stage he half-wakes to hear a car door bang and the murmur of voices, but as the car engine draws away so Ben slips back into sleep.

Poor Tom waits and waits. He thinks his entire life will be determined by whether or not his father was at, near, or even in the region of Kember. Dora sends him to bed, but he still sits up. Finally he creeps stealthily out of the house and makes his way by habit up the dark lane, for the clouds have long since shut out the moon. The call-box is bleakly empty as he knew it would be. He would like to kick the glass in, smash it up. He would like to, but doesn't. Instead he returns down the tunnel-like lane. The hedges stir and whisper. Tom feels a little afraid, not of real people but of ghosts that he doesn't believe in. Or does he? Yes he does. He can't help it. On his right he distinctly hears a movement, breathing. Tom panics. He runs. He is sure someone is coming after him; he can hear their steps. Too scared to look behind, he slithers and squelches through the muddy yard and pushes his way into the house. His aunt's door opens as he goes up the stairs.

'Tom. Where have you been?' Dora's teeth are out, Tom can tell by her speech.

'Nowhere,' he says, going into his own room.

Silence encloses the old house while the separate agitated thoughts of the occupants curl up into the night like wisps of smoke. Ron is the only one who, sleeping flat on his back. snores with inexorable regularity.

Rachel wonders how anyone can be as miserable as she is and still go on living. Joe has not come again tonight, and what about the money? Joe's absence is a sharp pain, like toothache; the money's absence is a steady dull hurt that is always there – a sore throat. Gradually the money ousts Joe and obsesses Rachel. Will Tamsin have enough sense to get it, and if so, how much? Will it be by Thursday when Rachel's boss is due to come? No wonder her fingertips are bare of nails. There are so many unknowns. She sits in bed, propped up against the wall with pillows, considering. Gradually Joe reassumes the uppermost position, bringing with him fresh anxieties so that Rachel starts to gnaw down the sides of her fingers. Is he now, at this very moment, out on the moor with Tamsin? Were his intentions not self-evident when he arrived with a car and not his bike? Rachel isn't sure. He had, after all, pointed out it was raining and it was not unusual for him to borrow a car. So it didn't really mean anything, did it? Rachel tears with primitive savagery at a tough piece of dry skin then looks sadly at the sore pink patch left behind. Well then, why hasn't he come back? Where is he? He isn't at his friend's: desperation has made Rachel swallow her pride and go down there to find out. She supposes he could be by now, but he wasn't an hour ago and the friend wasn't expecting him, he thought Joe was staying up at the garage. With high hopes Rachel returned to prepare food, make the place inviting, and wait. Waiting, for Rachel, is the worst thing in the whole world, yet it occupies a great part of her life. She sighs and unscrews the top of her pill bottle.

Joe is in the Meridan police station. Shortly after he left Tamsin he met the local constable head-on in a narrow stretch with only one light working. He was then asked to blow into the breathalyzer bag, which turned green. Since then it has transpired that Joe's borrowed car is not licensed for third party, and Joe is growing more and more hot; steamy hot. Why did he waste his money on Tamsin in the pub? If Tamsin had showed the effect of alcohol quicker he wouldn't have needed to drink as much himself. He hasn't really had much, not by usual standards, and how was he to guess he'd meet a copper head-on in the lanes? If he's fined, which he will be if not worse, who's going to pay the fine? Rachel? But he still owes her the money she borrowed for him from the till. She's been agitating for that back, fuck her. Impotence in his present position and rage at the unfortunate sequence of circumstance that has brought him to this pretty pass reduce Joe's always doubtful affection to nil. He feels that Rachel is completely to blame; Tamsin gets off more lightly. The thought of her touches Joe with sexual stirrings, whereas poor devoted Rachel touches him only as a provider, someone to bail him out when the time comes. Joe has complete faith in Rachel's passion for him. Lucky Joe.

Meanwhile the police still aggravate him with questions. What is he doing in that particular area at night in someone else's car? Where was he before? Joe is sharp, he watches his step, or tries to. He is careful to say a different pub and insist that he was alone. He gives his friend's address only. If Rachel were to find out about Tamsin it might alter her whole attitude over money.

Finally he is let go. At one a.m. he climbs in through Rachel's window. She has given up, locked up and gone to sleep. She wakes to find her dream come true as Joe's legs arrive on her bed followed by Joe. Soon she holds his cold, hard body in her warm arms and strokes his thick curly hair. She makes love to his body from tip to toe and he allows it. Lucky Rachel, she is as happy now as any woman can be.

I woke early and all the birds were singing. It gave me a kind of thrill, hearing the birds. Spring. Spring and me loving Joe made me feel great. I looked up at the window and it wasn't spring at all, the sky was dark as anything. My thoughts clouded over a bit too. There was that money Mum wanted. That was a chilling enough thought if my aunt was to catch me at it. I knew I'd have to try for it on the Wednesday because it was only on the Wednesday that she was off the place. Supposing she counted it and found some was gone, what then? I didn't care to think; it was a risk I'd have to take for my mum, because I'd determined on doing it for her to make up for my wronging her with Joe. I suppose some of my aunt's Methodism had rubbed off on me; not surprising after the way she dragged Tom and me along to chapel as kids. Anyway the truth of it was I felt guilty about Mum so I'd made this pledge with myself, I'd get her the cash. I planned it all the time I was getting dressed. I was still thinking about it when Tom and I walked up the lane for the school bus. Tom was thinking about something too, because neither of us spoke – not that we ever talk much but generally we argue about something or another.

While we were waiting for the bus to come Tom said quite sudden:

'Do you think Dad was out Kember?'

'Kember?' I said, staring at him. 'I never heard of Kember.'

'Out to the South Moor.'

'Dunno about that,' I said. 'What's the difference where he was?'

I felt sort of queer inside. How could he know where Dad had been? Could it be that someone had seen all of us out there and told Tom?

The bus came then. Tom sat at the back with his friends and I sat with mine. But Tom had got me worked up so I hardly heard a word Jan was telling me. Soon she realized and asked me what was up.

'I dunno,' I said. 'I just feel a bit funny.' After that she didn't talk any more and I looked out the window. I went back over the evening before, where we'd been and who could have seen us. We'd been in the pub at Kember, that was true enough, but how could Tom know? I decided I'd get hold of him at break and get it out of him.

So I did. I got him round the back of the boys' toilets.

'Tom,' I said, 'what do you know about Dad being out at Kember?'

'Was he?' Tom said, his eyes lighting up. He seemed terribly excited.

'I don't know,' I said. 'I'm asking you.'

'Oh.' His face fell a mile.

'Look,' I said. 'I want to know what you know about Kember. What put it in your head?'

'Nothing,' he said. I could see he was hiding something.

'Tom,' I said, 'I wasn't out at Kember, if that's what you mean. I never been there. I never even heard of it till you mentioned it just now.'

Tom gaped at me. 'I didn't say you was. It's Dad I want to know about.' I believed him then. I let him go.

'Ask him, I should,' I said, and left him. It still worked me up that Tom had even heard of Kember. I couldn't make it out.

What with that running round my head and the thought of getting the money, I didn't do very well in class. I got my essay back with C+ on it. That gave me a jolt; usually it was B or better. I slipped away soon as I could. I wanted to get along to Mum's. Maybe Joe'd be there. It seemed wrong somehow. Up till a few days back it'd been my mum I was keen to see. Now I was using her to see Joe. So I changed my plans completely and went home. It hurt watching that bus leave for Asherford without me, but it eased my guilty conscience. All the way home in the school bus I regretted it. I thought I'd die for wanting to see Joe.

Tom hadn't come back that evening. He was staying late for football coaching now the evenings were getting a bit lighter. I came in the yard and the first thing I saw was Dad. He'd got the front tyre off the tractor and was testing it to find the leak. He looked up when I came along. Since I'd got my private life, my new world that included Mum and Joe, I didn't have much to say to anyone out the farm. I'd never said much to Ron, nor Dad for that matter, but now I had to think careful before everything I said to my aunt as well, so as not to let anything out.

I thought I'd slip past him and get in the house but as I edged between him and the wall to pass the tractor he turned his head.

'Haven't you got a word for your dad, then?'

'Hullo,' I said.

Silence. The air started to hiss out the tyre.

'Puncture?' I said, kind of silly. It was obvious.

'Bloody thorn,' Dad said.

I started to edge my way on again.

71

'In a hurry this evening, aren't you?'

'I got work to do,' I said, waving my satchel. He straightened up.

'You didn't think about that yesterday – not coming home till all hours. How did you get home then, eh? Who was he?'

'I hitched,' I lied. 'Someone going through to Meridan.'

'Was he?' Dad said. He straightened up, grinning.

'I shouldn't mind a kiss myself from my own daughter I ain't hardly seen this past week.'

I felt sick, disgusted. I can't describe it.

'Not now, Dad,' I said. 'I'll give you one tonight.' To tell you the truth I was scared. I didn't know what was coming next till it came. He wiped his hands on the grease rag and dropped it. Then he caught my hand. I let him. I didn't know what else to do. Next thing, he moved forward and I stepped back tight to the wall. He put his mouth on mine and kissed me. Full. I saw his red heavy face coming close and shut my eyes to shut it out. Then he pressed his body up against mine and I could feel him hard as anything. I struggled free.

'Come off it, Dad,' I said breathless. 'Let me pass.'

So he stood back and let me go. I was shaking all over. I didn't know how to take it, as a joke or what. I knew what was going on all right. I wasn't that stupid. More than anything I think I was shocked, embarrassed, all of those things. I was more scared one of the others might have seen us than anything else. I felt such a fool, as though Dad was taking the mickey out of me.

I smoothed my hair and put my hands on my cheeks to cool them before I went in the house. Soon as I went in I saw my aunt was out. Her hat and beret were gone; she never went anywhere without them. I suppose that was why Dad had dared, he knew no one was round. Where was Ron? I wondered. I crossed the room and looked out the window the far side. I couldn't see anyone. Then the door opened and Dad came in. He glanced at me and went to wash his hands.

I felt myself tense up taut. He nodded at the stove.

'Tea?'

'Yes,' I said. I came across from the window and slid the kettle over. Dad sat down at the table and opened the *Farmer's Weekly*. I got the teapot, put some tea in it, got sugar and the milk jug, put them on the table, then stood waiting by the stove.

Dad looked up. 'How come you're home this evening instead of down Asherford?'

'It's only the odd evening I been down there,' I said.

He suddenly stared at me hard. 'Where is it you go down there, that's what I'd like to know. Eh?'

'I go down the Bawdens,' I said.

Dad laughed: 'That don't seem like what Dora'd call gospel truth,' he said, watching me close.

The kettle boiled. I poured it on the tea in the pot and put on the lid. I carried it across to the table and sat down. I was shaking; I could feel I was, but I couldn't stop it. I thought of running upstairs but somehow I couldn't and if I did I knew Dad'd come after me. The doors in the house didn't have locks. Then quick as could be he stretched his hand across and laid it on mine. I tried to pull mine out but he held it fast, so I stopped trying.

'Tell me,' he said. 'I want to know.'

'What do you want me to tell you?' I said, playing for time.

'Do you see her down there?' he said, very intense like.

There was a long pause. I heard the clock ticking and the sound of someone's chain-saw out across the field, maybe Ron's.

'Yes,' I said.

'Rachel?'

I nodded. I could hardly speak. I don't know why but I was near to tears. Everything seemed too much. I had so many confused feelings going round inside me, I didn't know how to act. Besides in a strange way it is very high-keyed to talk to your dad about your mother for the first time in your life. It was the way he said her name really knocked me; husky, reverent almost. I knew then he'd cared for her – once. I felt tears starting down my cheeks. With the hand he hadn't got I wiped them off.

He let go then, and sat back. 'I didn't mean to upset you, girlie,' he said quite gentle. That made me cry more. It always does if anyone is sympathetic. At the same time I dreaded he'd come round the table to me, but he didn't, he just tipped his chair back and rocked it on its back two legs, a thing Dora can't abide.

'Tell me about her then?' he said. 'How is she?'

'All right,' I said.

'Come on,' he said, 'you can tell me more'n that.'

So I did. I told him most of it up until Joe; I never mentioned Joe or any of that. Or the money.

'Where's Dora gone?' I said at the end.

'Over to Christine.'

'When'll she be back?'

'Should've been back afore now.'

'Will you tell her – about Rachel?'

Dad made no direct answer. 'She'll find out if she's not told,' he said. Then, 'She never was over-fond of your mum. I reckon they was two opposites. Rachel was one for the men, see, but not Dora. No, not Dora.' He laughed rather nastily, and that feeling of fear and disgust went through me again. I wanted to get away. At the same time I wanted to find out more about why my mother had left like she did.

'Didn't you care for each other?' I asked.

'Your mother didn't care for me. She was too good for me I dare say.' He looked at me. 'What does she have to say about it, then?'

'I haven't asked her,' I said. 'I didn't like to.'

Silence. I found myself listening to the clock's ticks again. I wanted to get out of there quick, I knew I ought to, but the longer I sat the more I couldn't move, and whichever way I crossed the room it meant passing Dad. So I went on sitting. Dad sat there, his arms on the table, blowing through his teeth under his breath. I guessed he was thinking about Mum. In the end I just had to move because I couldn't bear the tension, so I stood up. This jarred Dad back to now. He looked across at me, suspicious.

'Where are you going?'

'Nowhere,' I said. 'Upstairs.'

I started moving round the end of the table. I shifted a chair; it scraped the flags like a shriek. I could hear my own heart. I took a couple of steps for the stairs, next minute he was standing too.

'Wait.'

I stopped, rigid as Saul's wife.

'Yes?' I said. I wanted to humour him, keep things normal – as normal as they ever are. I faced him. He came towards me. I couldn't scream. I'm not a screamer, and anyway I was scared of anyone knowing what was going on. He got a hold of me, pulled me to him. Then his hands were going over me, fondling me. I couldn't bear it, I absolutely couldn't bear it, yet I stood there still as still. I didn't know what to do. When I felt his hands getting round the front of my legs, moving up, I pulled back.

'Dad,' I said, 'don't. I don't want you to.'

He was breathing hard. I pushed at him. I don't think he even felt it. He was fumbling with his trousers.

'Dad!' My voice rose. He couldn't be going to.

Then there was footsteps outside. He didn't seem to hear even then.

'Dad,' I said, frantic, 'there's someone coming.'

Then he did let me go. Ron came in with the chain-saw, plonked it down. Dad went back to his chair at the table. I went up the stairs quick. I lay down on my bed, my heart still thumping hard. I drew in deep breaths, I tried to think. First I thought I'd leave home, run off to my mother, then I knew I couldn't. She wouldn't have me, not permanent. Anyhow, Joe might have told her about me and him for all I knew. Gradually I calmed down. I saw the walls, the flaking paint, the spiders' webs, my quilt with flowers all over, and the carpet with the threads gone at the side, my bedroom slippers sticking out from under the bed, blue with fluffy balls on the toes . . . Bit by bit things straightened out, I just had to see to it I was never on my own with Dad, that's all I could do unless I was going to tell someone; and I wasn't, not in a million years. I thought I'd die sooner than tell anyone about this afternoon. Maybe Dad had a fit or something, maybe it wouldn't happen again. Already it was beginning to seem unreal. Maybe I'd imagined the half of it. Maybe it was just Dad trying to comfort me because I'd been crying.

Down below I heard voices. Dora was back. I hadn't done the calves; she'd be wild. I tied my hair back in a scarf so as not to get it milky when they slop you with their wet mouths, and went down.

Later the same evening Ron is out with his gun. Dora wants a rabbit, or if not a rabbit, a pigeon. Ron walks up over the nibbled-bare ground of the seeds field to the barley stubble beyond. The sheep raise their heads and shift a little closer to each other as he passes. Ron glances at them. Another two weeks to lambing, an early one may come at any time. He walks stealthily up the hedge to the gate and looks over: three rabbits. He raises his gun. The sheep run; the air reverberates. One rabbit runs on to its hole in the hedge. Ron goes through the gate and collects two dead corpses; one is still kicking and has to be knocked on the head. Carrying them with him, he starts back slowly, taking in the state of the hedges, machinery to be put into the barn, gate posts needed, stones fallen out of walls. Then his heart misses a beat. Towards him across the field is walking the unmistakable figure of the local copper. Inwardly Ron panics. Is his gun licence still valid? He stops, waits. The black figure of the copper advances like death, it seems to Ron. A few feet away, the constable stops.

'Afternoon, Mr Band.'

'Afternoon,' Ron mumbles.

'Been shootin'?' Constable Jenkins is not known for his

subtlety, only his cunning. Ron and he both eye the corpses.

'I came out here to ask you if you knowed anything about a young fellow called Joe Sanders. Not a local boy – one come down from up country.'

Ron looks at him blankly.

'Can't help you, copper.'

The constable doesn't believe this but doesn't expect much from Ron Band, who's long since been known as a 'closed one'.

'Think I'll walk back down the farm with you, see if any of them there can help me.'

Ron makes no comment as no comment seems needed. He and the constable walk, side by side but several yards apart, down the field towards the chimneys of Ventnor which just show above the dip of land into which it is settled.

Dora is 'straightening out' when she glances out of the window and sees Ron in the back yard with Constable Jenkins. For a few seconds she freezes, caught in motion like a figure in a relief, then she gives the alarm.

'Copper out in the yard with Ron, Ben.'

Ben doesn't need telling twice. He takes his rifle from beside the door and tucks it in the dark cupboard beneath some coats under the stair. He acquired it by doubtful means and certainly has no licence. Tamsin, who has come down and is at the table with her homework spread out, hasn't time to move before Ron and the constable enter. Tom follows behind them, an expression of consternation on his face. He has just got home. Which member of his family is about to be taken in jug? That all the Bands detest and distrust the police is evident in their silence and hostility. Only Dora makes an effort to placate the constable.

'Will you have a cup of tea, constable? I'm just making one.' She clatters the cups and saucers defensively.

'Thank you, Miss Band. I'll sit down if you don't mind.'

Constable Jenkins settles himself, takes out his notebook, looks all round the room, fixes his gaze on the frightened Tom. Are his powers of ESP a crime? Tom wonders. Is it him they have come for? 'If they want you for one thing, they'll shut you up for another' is the general attitude of the local people towards the hand of the law; and not without reason.

Dora places a large white cup and saucer before the constable, who picks up the teaspoon and helps himself to sugar from the bowl pushed towards him by Tamsin. He stirs amidst a complete silence broken only by the clock.

'Working hard?' Tamsin starts. She opens her mouth to answer but he's obviously lost interest. His eyes are fixed on Tom, who has turned white.

'Was that your bike out in the shed I passed?'

'Yes.' Tom's voice is nearly inaudible.

'Twisted out of line, by the look of it. Been in a crash?'

Dora butts in quickly.

'He crashed coming down the drive yesterday. He comes down that lane too fast, I'm always telling him. Hit a stone before the bridge.'

Tom's eyes grow larger as he listens to his aunt's story. The constable looks from one to the other.

'Is that right, young sir?'

'Yes,' mumbles Tom.

'Well, get it straightened out before I see you on the roads again.'

None of the Bands believe this is what the copper has come about. They wait, tensed, except for Ron who knows and stares owlishly.

'What I came about . . .' Constable Jenkins pauses enjoying the effect – 'is to ask if anyone here knows anything about a Joe Sanders.'

Silence. Tamsin doodles with her biro whirls of increasing sizes. She shades in the circle in the centre black.

The copper goes on. 'He was picked up along this lane Sunday night with only one headlight in a car he wasn't licensed to drive. Says he was on his own but someone else see'd the same car with a passenger in it earlier on.'

Silence. Tamsin lays down her biro and folds her hands. She fixes her eyes on the blue milk jug in front of her.

'You can't help me, can you, young lady?'

Tamsin feels trapped. How much does he know? She almost panics and admits, but her family's training overcomes her momentary desire for honesty.

'No,' she says, looking the constable in the eye, 'I don't know anything about him.'

Silence. The copper makes a laborious note in his book. Has he finished? Will he go? He puts his notebook in his pocket.

'Another thing,' he says. 'I came across some ponies straying on the road. They wouldn't be yours, would they?'

Ben looks up. Ben owns ponies he keeps on the moor and seldom sees more than once a year for the round-up.

'My ponies is safe up on Scarhill, constable,' he says firmly. 'My gates is good.'

'Check 'em up tomorrow.' The constable is brusque. He stands up. 'Thank you for the tea, Miss Band.'

Dora inclines her head and moves her lips in acknowledgement. The constable might well be an icon. Certainly as he moves towards the door, Dora is breathing a prayer of thanks. She shuts the door behind him and watches him walk away through the glass pane put there for this purpose, then turns on Tamsin.

'What have you been up to, bringing the police in here?'

Tamsin, cornered, mutters, 'He gave me a lift back. Least I s'pose that's who it was.'

'Who is he?' Dora's not going to let it go.

'A friend of Denise's,' Tamsin lies.

'A friend of Rachel's.' Ben brings it out.

Dora starts; it is her turn to change colour. She looks accusingly at Tamsin.

'Is that where you been?'

'Yes.' Tamsin is defiant now. What else can she be?

79

'You mean you been telling us one thing and doing another? All this while you been down Asherford along of Rachel?'

Tamsin is silent. Dora looks furiously at Ben. Isn't he going to do anything, say anything? Apparently not.

'Haven't you got anything to say to her, Ben?'

Ben has no wish to cross Tamsin unduly.

'You can't prevent the girl seeing her mother, Dora,' he says treacherously. Dora could kill him. After all he's said!

'I'm not saying any more,' says Dora. 'Just don't expect nothing from me in the future. I done my bit and I see it's all been wasted.' She blows her nose twice.

The tension in the room is pronounced. Tamsin starts to say something but Dora cuts her short.

'Don't speak to me. I don't want to hear any more.' She hurries across the room to the stairs. As she opens the door she blows her nose again and exits.

Ron goes through to the larder with the rabbits. Ben shuts his eyes. Tom stares at Tamsin. He feels sorry for her. He's glad he's not in her shoes. He looks across at his father and wonders if he dares ask him about Kember. He decides not.

Rachel's alarm clock goes at eight a.m. She gets out and leaves Joe asleep beside her. Humming blithely she makes herself coffee, dresses herself in dungarees – her garage uniform – and goes out to meet the world.

Joe wakes about mid-day. He lies contemplating his unhappy situation. Not only is he likely to have his licence taken away but he will certainly be in for a heavy fine. Bugger Tamsin. If it hadn't been for her he wouldn't have borrowed the car and none of this would have happened. And all for what? He should have known better than to expect much from a sixteen year old. She's appealing, though, he's in no doubt about that. He tries to concentrate on money; he'll have to have some, he'll have to twist Rachel's arm. Surely she can borrow a bit more from the cash-desk without too much risk?

Joe dresses himself. As he pulls on his skin-tight jeans a plan begins to form. He will get away from this aimless, unemployed life; he will go to London. If there is no employment there (which he doubts: there must be jobs for anyone willing to do them) at least there will be life. He should be able to slip away unknown, nameless into the vast metropolis where it will take weeks for the police to trace him, and by which time, if they ever do, he will have money enough to pay. Having decided to act, Joe feels much better. He whistles and combs his hair carefully, then saunters out and takes over the pumps while Rachel goes to the shops.

Between one thirty and two p.m. Alf takes over while Rachel and Joe have their dinner. Joe puts it to Rachel: they'll go to London, they'll need a little cash for the journey, not much, they'll soon both be in part-time work. Rachel looks at him in amazement. Why? She has a job and somewhere to live here. There is nothing to guarantee either in London. Her friends are here too. Joe flies into one of his black moods, a kind of cold rage that Rachel has learnt to dread. He might have known there was no point even discussing it with her; she's older than him and therefore set in her ways. Rachel bravely probes. Desperate because he needs her money if not her support, Joe tells her about the previous night. Rachel thanks her lucky stars Tamsin was not with him when he was picked up. She also makes a mental note of how long Joe and Tamsin must have been on the moor together, although Joe makes the excuse of pulling the 'old bugger's car' out of the ditch, which she doesn't believe.

They reach an impasse. Joe is furious, uncertain and abusive. Rachel feels hopeless, deflated. Worst of all she feels sure Joe has made love with Tamsin. Her jealousy is directed against neither Tamsin nor Joe; it simply eats her up, allows her no peace. Her night's happiness rises from her hands like a carrier pigeon, circles and flies away. Will she ever see it again? And then the money – the money is always there like a toothache. Tamsin must, must bring her the £50. Joe's suggestion of borrowing further money is out of the question. She will lose Joe, but then hasn't she already – to Tamsin? But if she went to London with him perhaps it would be different. He can't be that nuts about Tamsin or he wouldn't want to go. She consoles herself with this last thought, feels better; she goes out and fills the tank of the next customer's car with her thoughts already in London.

'You'll take her, won't you?' Joe asks.

'Take who?' Rachel knows but refuses to accept.

'Tamsin. She's your daughter, isn't she?'

'She won't leave the farm.'

'That's not what she told me. Sounds a dump for someone her age.'

'She's not finished school.'

'She will of, in a month.'

'I thought you were talking about the end of the week?'

'I am.'

'Well then?' Rachel triumphs, changes key. 'You don't care about me, do you Joe? Tamsin's the one.'

'Course I care about you. Tamsin's a kid. I felt sorry for her, her just having found you an' all. Seems tough on her, leaving her so quick.'

'Yes,' Rachel agrees sadly. She's uncertain whether her sadness is for Tamsin or herself. For both, she decides.

'I'll ask her when she comes down Thursday,' she says. Then adds, 'There's Tom.'

'Bugger Tom,' says Joe. 'We can't have the whole fucking family.'

'No,' agrees Rachel. Indeed, she has not yet seen Tom. Perhaps it's better she never should. Rachel indulges in momentary self-pity, or is it pity for Tom?

Joe, who is on his way to his friend, leaves. Rachel automatically resumes her task, takes pay from her last customer, who has helped himself, and gives him the change.

'Tom?' I said. Both of us were out in the buildings hand-feeding the calves. Tom was in the next-door stall.

'Can you hear me?' I asked. I waited to be sure. 'I'm

82

taking the day off tomorrow,' I said, 'and I don't want you to say nothing, go putting your foot in it.'

He didn't answer. 'What do you want, then?' I asked.

'The lamp,' he said. 'I still ain't had it.'

'But with your bike all buckled what's the use?' I asked.

'I still want it,' he said, obstinate. That's his main quality, obstinacy.

'OK,' I said. 'If you promise not to let on. I'm saying the day off's for the top form only. A revising day for our exams.'

'Yeah,' he said. Then, 'Why?'

I'd expected that'd come. He's curious too. Nosy.

'I got to do something for my mother,' I said.

'You promised you'd take me to see her.' Tom was aggrieved.

'I will,' I said. 'Maybe next week.'

'Promise?'

'Yes,' I said. Next week seemed years away. By then I'd have this money worry off my hands. So that settled tomorrow, in part. The other part, which hammered away down inside me and I tried not to think about, was that I'd be on my own with Dad. Right now I pushed it out my mind. I had to get the money.

Back in the house we washed out the buckets and took off our boots. The wind had gone cold, east. My fingers were numb as anything and I went in to warm them over the stove. Ron was there bent over a box. I looked over his shoulder and saw a lamb looking like it was going to die.

'I didn't know you'd started,' I said.

'No more did I,' he said. 'But two of 'em come just now.'

'Where's the other?'

'In the shed along with his mother. This here's the weak 'un.'

It certainly looked like it; it had that I'm-going-to-die kind of bleat. I went up to my room. I put on the light and got under the bedclothes for the cold. I wanted to plan exactly. Dora'd be gone at ten a.m. on the bus. Ron'd be out most of the time especially if there was lambs – a stroke of good fortune for me, that was. Dad was the problem. I reckoned in this weather he'd be sat in the kitchen, and the door to the office led off of the kitchen. I'd just have to risk it, sit around, and take my chance, do my revision down there. A kind of fear I couldn't describe started welling up when I thought of being in the kitchen with Dad, but I told myself if the worst came to the worst I was quicker than Dad; I could get away. Even so I felt a kind of panic and the longer I thought about it the worse panic I got into. I can't do it, I thought, there's no way. Ten minutes later I was decided. I took three 5p's and went out the house and up the lane to the call-box.

The wind was whistling round, bending the trees in the hedges. It blew through my clothes as though I was naked. Poor bloody lambs, I thought, if they were born tonight, they'd be stiff before they even tried to stand. I struggled up the last stretch which was steep and faced straight into the east wind. A few minutes later I was in the call-box. I dialled, waiting with 5p. Mum answered.

'Mum.'

'Yes. Oh it's you, Tamsin.'

I hesitated. Then I said, sort of helpless, knowing as I said it it wasn't going to work: 'I don't think I can do it.'

I heard the silence the other end. Then Mum's voice came back sharp and anxious.

'You promised. There's no other way.' There was a pause, then she went on: 'You'll have it back the day after, I've told you. It's simply borrowing it for a few hours, that's all it is.'

'But Mum—' I began. She interrupted.

'I thought you'd do it for me – this one thing. It's the only thing I've ever asked of you, Tamsin. You know what it'll mean to me.'

Pause.

'Tamsin?'

'Yes,' I said.

'I thought you'd gone. Joe was talking about going to London . . . and taking you. If you'd like to come.'

My heart gave a little bound of joy. London! To go to London was a dream I'd had for the last three years.

'When?' I said.

'End of the week.'

I couldn't believe it. Then I thought of school and my heart sank. I knew I couldn't go.

'I've got my exams,' I said.

'I know, but we'd get set up and you'd join us just as soon as they finish.'

'Yes,' I said weakly. It all sounded so possible and impossible.

'But I have to have the money first.' Pause, then: 'For God's sake, Tamsy, try for me.' Mum sounded desperate. The pips went.

'All right,' I said.

'Thanks.' The relief in her voice seemed to come along the line and touch me. We were cut off. I put the receiver down and went back out into the east wind. My feet were numb, I felt numb altogether. By the time I reached the house I was nearly crying with cold.

My aunt looked at me curiously. 'I had to find out what work we're s'posed to give in tomorrow,' I muttered. She let it pass. I ran the bath. The water was tepid, so I boiled two kettles to add to it.

Dora, with two weighty shopping bags, is making for Mabs Mellors'. The traffic waits while she crosses the pedestrian crossing, then hastens on with a grinding of gears and hot puffs of exhaust.

Dora pushes open the door of the café, newly decorated in green and gold, and looks round for Edith. She sees her waving from the far corner, surrounded by carrier bags and her own shopping trolley. Dora wonders that Edith is not embarrassed to occupy so much floor-space; she herself couldn't do it. She threads her way through the tables and arrives beside Edith, climbs between Edith's spilling bags and takes a seat.

'I thought you were never coming.'

'There seemed more of 'em than usual round the stalls.' Dora pushes a wisp of grey hair under her woollen beret. She is glad to be sitting; her feet get tired walking on pavements.

She wonders how Edith can manage, overweight as she is.

'I've ordered tea. I didn't know whether you'd want anything to eat.' Edith looks longingly at the cakes displayed beside her.

Dora takes off her woollen gloves. 'A cup of tea will do me, thank you.'

Edith looks across at her resentfully. A mean spindle she must be to live with! She feels sorry for those poor kids . . . She checks herself. Dora is, after all, her best friend. Where would she be without Dora to meet in Mabs Mellors' on a Wednesday? Meeting Herbert Bawden in The Red Lion? Well, why not – it *could* happen.

The tea arrives. Edith pours out. Dora takes her cup and drinks with relief – it is what she needed. Edith waits expectantly. She knows Dora has something to tell her; it is simply a question of getting her started. Meanwhile precious time is passing. Edith feels forced to prompt.

'Heard any more of Rachel, then?'

'Tamsin's been seeing her, I do know that.' Dora wipes her lips and pours a further cup for both of them. 'I feel I've done my bit,' she says. 'If she's determined on going down Rachel's then I'm not one to stop her. You can't keep a girl from her mother.'

'But,' says Edith, 'what effect will it have on her, I mean to say?'

Dora sighs. 'I can't think it will benefit her, that's what I said to Ben. And he's of the same opinion. But he won't do anything, so it's not for me to prevent her.' Dora doesn't care to say that there is no means by which she *can* prevent Tamsin. She wonders if Edith has news, but hesitates to ask outright. Instead she lapses into silence. Edith's eyes brighten. She clears her throat, pushes her cup a little to one side.

86

'How about this young lad, then? Joe Sanders, the one the police picked up in Meridan last Sunday night.'

Dora tenses. She waits.

'I heard he's the one lives along of Rachel down Asherford.'

Dora adds water to the pot. That's why the constable came questioning them, she supposes, but refrains from mentioning it to Edith. She does not want the whole area to know the Bands are being questioned.

'What's more,' Edith continues, 'it's spoken around that your Tamsin was seen in the car with him on the Sunday afternoon, leaving Asherford.'

This last shot goes home. Dora's hand wobbles as she replaces the cup in the saucer; the tea slops.

'Who saw her?'

'Mary Sheen in the hardware store over the bridge.'

'I've known her be wrong before now.' Dora doesn't really believe that Mary Sheen is wrong. It all makes too much sense.

'It's difficult for you, I can see that.' Edith's voice mellows in sympathy. 'Still, I think if I was you I should take a firmer hand. I should say to the girl, "Either you stay with me or you go to your mother, you can't have your cake and eat it".' Reminded, Edith glances at the cake counter again. Cream oozes from an eclair.

'Yes,' agrees Dora meekly, but she is afraid that if she said this Tamsin might go, and she, Dora, cannot face the thought of Ventnor without Tamsin. If only she could convey to Tamsin how much she means to her, but that is the one thing poor chapel-raised Dora cannot do: she cannot express her feelings; nor can Ron, nor indeed can any of the senior Bands. Look at Ben. Wicked Ben some people would say – poor Ben, others. The fact is Ben is the only one of the Bands who makes an occasional sally into self-expression. Usually it is disastrous.

So Dora sits and sips tea knowing that she will be able to tick Tamsin off, to scold, to punish even, but not to say to Tamsin, 'I love you. I don't want you to leave me for your

87

unreliable mother.' Perhaps Tamsin is lucky that Dora cannot impose this final emotional blackmail on her.

Edith carries on. She would do this and this and this. Dora hardly hears. She is truly worried. Will Tamsin become implicated with Joe, Rachel and the police? What is going on, what has been going on? She must get back home, try to find out. Edith sees she has overdone it. Too late she tries to soothe and pacify, to no effect. Dora is already on her feet collecting her bags, excusing herself for not staying longer. Edith points out that the bus goes the same time as usual. Dora says she hopes for a lift from the Barnetts up at the cross. She pays her bill at the counter, waves gaily, she hopes, to Edith left desolate amidst her purchases, and hurries out. She is sweating; she breathes deeply. Has it suddenly gone milder?

Grasping her bags, she starts off for the car park where she knows the Barnetts have left their pick-up.

Wednesday is the third day Joe has been hanging round the garage doing nothing. Rachel doesn't mind; on the contrary, she would be pleased if he wasn't so short tempered and edgy. She supposes it is because he is waiting for his summons. Certainly all he does each day is walk down to Mike's house to see if there's any post and once a week go into Meridan to collect his dole money. Mike has gone to Cornwall in search of work, so that's why Joe is disconsolate, in part. For the rest, he's fed up with Asherford, fed up with bumming around and no work, fed up with Rachel – though he can't say so while she's supporting him. So he spends most of the day on the settee reading motor magazines and endlessly smoking cigarettes provided by Rachel. Occasionally he wanders out and takes over from her at the pumps, but more often she comes in, has a fag and discusses their escape to London – for that's how she sees it. Rachel has never learned from experience that another person's grass only looks greener. Perhaps her optimism is part of her charm.

She leans forward now, fag in mouth, for Joe to light it,

then perches on the arm of her chair. Alf is on the pumps. Joe is stretched on the settee.

Rachel sighs nervously. She always feels nervous when speaking to Joe. He has that power, conveyed by his look, to make most of what she says sound stupid. Her funny stories that make others roar never sound funny told to Joe. She understands perfectly the meaning of tongue-tied.

'Have you made up your mind, then?' She tries not to sound eager, casual rather.

Joe looks at her pityingly. 'Made up *my* mind some time back. I thought it was you didn't know what you wanted.'

'Joe –' Rachel tries a seductive, how-can-you-misunderstand-me tone ' – you know all I want is to shift along with you. I thought I'd made that clear.'

Yes, but does Joe want Rachel along with him, permanently? He lights up another fag. He's got to have her at the start, that's sure, because of the money. Then suddenly, like a vision, a flash of inspiration, Joe has an idea about the money. He knows exactly where the keys of the till are kept. Why not? He goes on smoking in silence. Rachel is talking.

'See, it's like this. I'll have to give in my notice end of this week. Then the following I'll get my pay plus the one week extra, plus my holiday pay due – the holiday I didn't take back in the summer.' Of course she didn't, she never left the pumps in case she missed a glimpse of Joe when he came to fill up his motorbike. Her heart gives a quick throb at the delicious memories: Joe on his bike turning in the yard, Rachel tanned, young it seemed to herself, radiant, the wind blowing her hair, standing casually inviting like the Regent Girl advert, waiting to serve him; Joe circling, drawing in; those precious, brief, fatuous words exchanged; Joe laughing at her, tearing out of the yard at a breakneck speed, zigzagging, waving to make an impression. Oh happy days! Rachel jerks herself back to the present.

'So you see, if you can wait another week, well ten days, say, we'd have a good bit more.'

Joe sees that but he can't wait, not for the familiar, too-adoring middle-aged Rachel. Recently he's come in for a good few jibes over associating with Rachel. It has hurt Joe's pride. He thinks nostalgically of Tamsin. Tamsin is a different kettle of fish. Tamsin has the looks (if not the performance) to make her escort envied. Joe stretches himself further along the settee and yawns. Diane had been a bit of all right too, but her dad had put his foot down. Joe wishes Rachel would get back to the pumps; a plan is forming in his mind that can crystallize only in Rachel's absence. He needs peace to think. Rachel is still talking.

'I get paid on the Friday week, so there's nothing to stop us going up on the Saturday . . . that is, if you want to.'

Fuck it, you stupid woman, I'm going at the end of this week, Joe thinks. They'll have me inside if we don't go till you suggest. He stands up. He feels imprisoned in the small room. He'll have to get out. He looks belligerently at Rachel, who takes the hint, removes herself from her perch, and goes out to the pumps. Alf gives over gladly. Customers and dealing with metric money frighten him.

As Joe goes out he passes Rachel getting change from the till. She locks it every night and keeps the key in her dungarees pocket hung on the back of her bedroom door. Once a week, on Fridays, her boss comes and collects the cash, which he either pockets or takes to the bank, Joe doesn't know which. What Joe does know is that he himself must take the money at the end of the week, Thursday night, say, when it will have collected up a bit. There isn't that much trade at this time of year. Joe knows nothing about the £50 Tamsin is planning to borrow from her aunt Dora's drawer.

Through the partition I heard Tom get up and go down. I heard them all beneath in the kitchen, then the door banged – that would have been Tom going for the school bus. The door went again; that'd be Ron. Then my aunt's voice shouted up the stairs.

'Tamsin? Aren't you going in today?'

I heaved myself out of the warmth on to the cold boards. I took my dressing-gown off of the door and went down. My aunt looked at me with disapproval. If there's one thing she hates it's anyone coming down in the morning not dressed.

'Are you ill, then?' she asked, seeing I wasn't.

'No,' I said. 'I'm staying home to revise.'

She looked even more disapproving and suspicious with it.

'Get dressed, then,' she said, 'and have your breakfast. You won't get anything done lying round half the morning in bed.'

I sat down and helped myself to cereal. I knew she'd have to go soon. The Taverston bus was at the top of the lane at nine forty-five.

'Won't you miss your bus?' I asked.

She looked anxiously at the clock. She was always early and had to wait around for it. Now she put her basket and purse on the table, took her coat and beret off the back of the door and put them on in front of the mantel mirror. I ate my cereal and watched. I didn't feel nervous any more; I felt fortified. I thought I'd go through it like Macbeth, only I wouldn't make a botch-up and start giving myself away by what I said. I'd be perfectly cool and deliberate, and get on with it. Dad wasn't around, I was pleased to see. I couldn't believe my luck.

My aunt opened her purse to check her money. For a moment I froze. Supposing she took the key in her purse with her? But no, why should she? She never had before. I went on munching.

'Where's Dad?' I asked casually. My aunt was counting and making some calculations, so she didn't answer at once. When she did, she didn't seem to be concentrating.

'Gone out,' she said. 'He'll be back later. There's a pie in the fridge. You can give him his lunch, and Ron. I'll be back on the three o'clock bus.'

As if I didn't know.

Then Ron came in.

My heart sank. I'd thought as soon as Dora was gone I'd have the place to myself and be able to get on with what I had to do, but no such luck. Ron had some cogs and knobs in a cardboard box which he placed in front of himself. He got out a rag and started slowly and laboriously cleaning each bit.

My aunt left.

I cleared my plate away and made myself some tea. I gave Ron a cup too, I had to.

'Long job?' I asked, standing above him sipping my tea.

'No,' he said, 'not long. Fiddly.'

'Not long' meant nothing with Ron; it could have meant an hour, a day, a week.

'What is it?' I asked.

'Part of the gear-box out the small tractor,' he said.

'So you mean you won't be able to use it today?'

'I'll have it back in by after dinner,' he said. I had got the information I wanted. Ron would be here half the morning at least, before he started to reassemble. My luck was out. I went upstairs and got dressed. I collected an armful of books, took them down and spread them all over the kitchen table. At least I wouldn't be shut up there on my own with Dad, I thought, that was one thing to the good.

I couldn't work, though. I couldn't concentrate. Every moment I was looking up at the clock. Every time Ron went out I wondered if he'd be gone long enough for me to get through in the office and do what I had to. Once he went out and I saw him lying on his back half under the tractor. Now, I thought. I wished I knew where Dad was, but decided I'd take the risk. I went across the room and had just got the office door handle turned when Ron came back in. I let it go quick and shifted back to the table. He didn't notice but it was a near thing. No one ever goes in that room but my aunt. He'd have been bound to smell a rat.

I sat down again. I was sweating under the armpits; I could smell myself. Rather sweet it was, unpleasant. I guessed it was nerves. I tried to read the print in front of me but it blurred and danced. If it kept still I didn't take it in, just read the same paragraph over and over again. Then Dad came in. I don't know where he came from but I knew all right once he was there. I didn't have to look, I could feel him. If there was one thing I hated it was sitting in the same room as Dad. I couldn't relax, he made me edgy. Any time was bad, but today was terrible. There I was stuck with the two of them. I began to despair. I wasn't going to get a chance at all. There was nothing I could do but go on sitting there staring down at my books.

Then Ron went out.

'Finished?' I asked as he passed me.

'Oughter be,' he said, pushing his feet in his boots.

The door closed behind him. So that left me and Dad. Dad had his feet up and his eyes closed. He looked as though he was settled in for the day.

'It isn't raining, is it?' I asked.

He opened his eyes. They looked very small, I thought, and his skin very red. Drink, I supposed – I mean the redness was drink.

'No, it ain't raining,' he said.

I knew he knew I meant, 'Why don't you go out and do something?' But he wasn't going to take no notice. I wished I hadn't spoken, for now he sat watching me: cat and mouse. I really did feel like a mouse, waiting and waiting for the cat to look away so I could creep for the hole I wanted.

After a bit I had to do something. I couldn't stand to go on sitting there looking at my books, so I thought I'd get the lunch. I got the pies out the fridge and put them in a tin in the bottom oven.

'Early, ain't it?' Dad seemed almost to be laughing at me. It was uncanny – as though he knew I was waiting to get rid of him. He was sat right near the stove and every time I went to the oven I had to go right close to him. Once I was bending down and he caught my skirt and lifted it.

'Don't,' I said, jerking it away. I knew I'd gone red as him. I hated him. He laughed.

'What's the matter?' he said. 'Can't a man look at his own maid?'

'I shan't get the dinner,' I said, 'unless you let me alone.'

'I'm letting you alone, aren't I? I ain't laid a finger on you save for lifting your skirt.'

Him saying that made me flush again. Yet I could see what he meant. He was my father so I supposed he had a right to behave like he did with me – that's how we were reared to think. I don't think we were unusual. I think a lot of kids grew up thinking just that way. Still, I took the precaution of calling Ron before I went back to the oven again. Ron came in and washed his hands. I put the pies on the table, and bread and butter and pickle, and we had our meal. Dad and Ron had draught cider, I had water. I made a pot of tea to finish up with.

Ron went out almost directly.

'I'm off,' he said. 'I'll be in Cleaver Piece.' Cleaver Piece was the top field next the road.

'Will you be long,' I asked, 'in case anyone comes?'

There's sometimes salesmen or someone delivering something but really I was thinking of Dad.

'Till four,' he said, and I knew he'd probably be later. He went without even glancing at Dad. He never seemed to expect Dad to do anything. I didn't know how he had patience with him. I couldn't have had if I was Ron.

Dad shut his eyes and went back to sleep. I could see he wasn't going to move, not before Dora got back and disturbed him. Soon he began not exactly snoring but breathing real noisy with his mouth open. He sounded asleep good and proper. I didn't know what to do. Should I creep through now and risk it, or wait and hope? After a while, hoping seemed pointless. I stood up and made a lot of noise bustling about. I clapped the kettle over, to see if he'd wake, but his breathing went on noisy as ever and he didn't shift a bit. So I went to the office door, quick, just like that. All the time I was repeating prayers to keep Dad from waking. I undid the door, it made a noise I'd never noticed before, and went in. Dad hadn't shifted. I walked across to the desk, almost like I was in a trance, opened the drawer and took out my aunt's bank-notes all done up in bundles with a rubber-band round them. She did them in lots of ten. I knew that because I'd watched her count them at the kitchen table often enough. So I picked out five lots now, then paused. What was I to do with them? I couldn't think and I had to hurry, so I put them down while I closed the top of the desk. I was so nervous I suppose I was clumsy, because I thought it was down when it wasn't and it slipped out my fingers and dropped the last inch. The noise it made sounded like a gun going off to me. I was sure it'd wake Dad. I waited frozen with fright for him to come. But after a minute or two he still didn't, so I thought it was all right. I took the notes I'd pushed under the blotter and started for the door. As I came round it I was brought up short. Dad was standing right in front of me, waiting for me.

Guilt must have been written all over my face, which was daft, because I don't think he had any idea what I was up to even though I was holding the notes. He just stood grinning at me, kind of horrible.

'Can I get past, please,' I said, at last. I took a step forward.

He put his hand out, barring the way more.

'What you been doing in the office?' he asked.

'I was looking for a ruler,' I said. 'That's all.'

'I don't see no ruler,' he said. He stepped forward.

'What you got held there? Show us.'

'I was . . . borrowing a bit,' I said. 'I'm paying it back Friday.'

'Borrowing? Pinching more like. I'll lay my last pound Dora doesn't know. Does she?' he said, sharp.

'No,' I said. 'But I'll tell her.'

'She won't let you go taking from her private desk. What are you thinking about, girlie? That's farm income you got there.'

He took a step forward. I stepped back. He took another step. I was back in the office now and he was stood right in the doorway.

'Let me keep it, Dad,' I pleaded. 'Just this one time. I swear I'll pay it back Friday.' I was scared now, scared in a different way. It was the look in Dad's eyes. He came right on into the office and closed the door behind him. There we were together in a room no bigger than the piano practice rooms at school. And still he came on forward and I backed away. I went on backing until I came up against the wall. The other wall was on my right and the desk, a big oak one, was on my left. I was trapped. Dad came up close. I couldn't stand to look at him so I turned my face away.

'What's the matter then?' he murmured. 'Don't you like your dad?'

His breath was hot in my face, horrible. He took hold my chin and pulled it round to him. Then he reached for my fingers and took the notes. He counted them and looked at me. He chuckled. I hated the sound of it. 'You little thief,' he said. 'You little devil. You're the same blood as your mother, that's what you are.'

'It's for her,' I said. 'That's why I have to have it.'

'Yes,' he said, 'you're a lot like her. You look like she did at your age.' He seemed to have lost interest in the notes. He laid them on the desk. It was me he was looking at. I knew any moment he was going to touch me and I couldn't move for the fear of it.

'Tell you what,' he said. 'Give your dad a kiss and I won't say nothing about it to Dora nor Ron. How's that for a bargain?'

I reckoned whatever I said wouldn't make him stop what he had in mind, so I tried to smile.

'Promise?' I said. 'Promise you won't say to the others?'

He tipped my face up to his. 'I promise,' he said, kind of thick. Then his thick wet lips came down on my mouth and he put his hands on me, moving his body in close, breathing heavy. I hated him. I hated myself. I thought I'd be sick from disgust. Finally he let me go and I took the money and walked out. I was shaking all over, scared silly Dad'd come after me. I went out the front door and up to the hay loft above the calve-sheds. From where I was I could see

96

anyone come out the front door and I thought I could hide the money till I had the chance to get to Asherford. I wanted somewhere quiet to think, and the hay loft seemed as good a place as any, safe too. It was the kind of loft that's at ground level at the back so you can walk in, and about twelve-feet or more off the ground on the side looking over the yard and house. It was built into the hill. First I clambered right to the back of the barn and pushed the money in the wall behind a loose stone I pulled out and replaced; then I lay on my stomach where I could look out and see if Dad were to come out; at the same time I could make plans about getting the money to Mum. I was dead scared, but at the same time I had a sense of triumph over getting the money. Everytime I thought of Dad up close it filled me with a horrible sick feeling, so I concentrated on the money. There was no means of getting it down to Asherford till tomorrow because there wasn't a bus, so somehow I'd got to get through the rest of the afternoon and evening keeping my fingers crossed my aunt didn't go looking in the drawer. I didn't think Dad'd say anything for fear of what I might say; I thought I was safe in that way. But for the time being, I had to stay where I was. I couldn't go in till Dora or Ron were back, that was for certain. Tom wouldn't get back off the school bus till after my aunt. I didn't know the time but I thought I must have at least an hour to wait, maybe more. The house was quiet and after a while I got tired of watching the door. I rolled over on my back and watched the white doves up above on the roof trusses fanning their tails at each other and walking up and down along the ties. A third one was at the far end watching, she didn't seem to fan her tail so I thought perhaps she was the female and the others were fighting over her – that's what it seemed like. Then I started planning for the next day again. It seems crazy now I think back, but I must have gone to sleep. The hay was comfy and I hadn't slept at all the night before for worrying about the money, so I suppose that's how it was. I woke with a jerk not remembering where I was and sure I'd heard something. I turned over. Dad was standing on the bales looking down on me.

At the top of Ventnor lane Tom is still waiting for the school bus when his aunt comes panting up the hill. The market bus arrives promptly and bears Dora Band away. Tom watches the green beret recede through the back window. He continues to wait. After he-doesn't-know-how-long he decides he's missed it, and joyfully, if rather guiltily, he retraces his way back down the lane. At the entrance to the yard he pauses. If he goes in and says he's missed the bus he'll be set to mucking out the piggery, whereas what he would really like to do is fish. Accordingly, he goes round the back of the yard buildings and into the lean-to built up against the house and known as the 'dairy'. The house is silent. Tom feels safe. The dairy is divided from the rest of the house by two doors and a passage. He'll hear easily enough if someone starts coming through. Tom looks up to where Ron's trout rod is temporarily kept, laid along wooden supports projecting from the wall. His eyes shine. He reaches it, lifts it down and runs his hands up and down it lovingly. Ron allows him to borrow it occasionally, but the trouble'll come if he's found out of school. Standing on tiptoe he feels along a shelf above his head for the tin box of flies. His fingers close round the cold metal, he takes it down and opens it. With mounting excitement he studies the array of varying flies. He strokes the bright colours of the big salmon flies, but finally settles for a small, inconspicuous ginger fly. He removes it from the clip, knots it carefully on to the cast, and replaces the box.

Now, furtively nursing the long rod, he lets himself out of the outside door which lets light into the dairy through absent glass panes, and walks along the side of the buildings. Keeping well tucked under the hedges, Tom makes his way along the fields towards the stream. It's small for holding fish but Tom consoles himself that it's big enough for sea trout to run up in the autumn. Often enough he and

Ron have been down with a torch at night to net them. Then Ron has sold them and made a bit for all, that's what his aunt said. Same as over the foxes' skins.

Once Tom is well away from the farm, he relaxes. He climbs over the boundary fence on to the adjoining farmer's ground where the trees thin out and it's easier to cast. He's not afraid of being caught. Arch Huxtable never goes far from his buildings. A pony kicked him in the thigh years ago and saw to that.

So this end of Arch's land is a sheep-grazed wilderness. Wrens, unused to disturbance, tick their anxiety all round Tom as he sits on a mound, takes a tin of grease out of his pocket and sets to greasing his line.

Two and a half hours later Tom returns the way he's come – with the rod but without the fly. Sadly it is high up on the tip of a branch of alder even Tom's agility has been unable to reach. The cast, too, is broken. Feeling less happy at the thought of Ron's anger, Tom lets himself into the same back door of the dairy, replaces the rod on its support, and gets a new cast out of a further tin. While he is trying to unknot the broken cast he hears voices from the office, which surprises him. No one except Auntie ever goes in the office and she's gone down the market. He has seen her go for himself. Curious, he listens. It sounds like his dad's voice and Tamsin's. But the importance of his own task makes him dismiss the oddity of his dad and Tamsin being on his aunt's sacred territory. Soon the voices cease. A few minutes later he hears Tamsin run up the stairs. Later still the front door slams. Tom tenses nervously. Whoever it is could come round by way of the dairy. But no, no one approaches. He continues struggling with the cast. Finally he completes its replacement, cautiously reels in the pulled-out line, and slots the reel back on the rod. His task complete, he looks round, wondering how he can fill the remaining hours until it will look as though he has returned off the bus. The house is out of the question. He's bound to be found by Tamsin if no one else. He eyes up the buildings. The hay loft opposite gazes back at him with a doorless, vacant eye. The sound of someone shifting about in the house – almost certainly his dad because the tractor's gone so that means Ron is up in the fields – makes up Tom's mind. Taking one last longing glance at the rod, Tom lets himself out the door and crosses the gate between the yard and the field lane to the comparative safety of the back of the calve-sheds. Once there he hesitates, undecided. He doesn't want to waste his valuable day in a hay loft. Better go up the field behind to the coppice and cut out a new catapult. Tom's knife bulges reassuringly from his pocket.

So that's what he does. He scrambles up the ground to the coppice, selects his forked hazel, and sits himself on the ground to work on it. From where he is, he can see right through the big double doorway of the hay loft to the white square of sky framed by the doorway on the far side. He can also keep an eye on the lane and road, so he will see when his aunt returns. Tom relaxes. He has achieved an ambition he's long been nursing, that of fishing quite on his own with a real rod, and has cast a fly with some success even if the fish aren't taking. The pale, watery sun that has come and gone all day shines more brightly now although it is low in the sky. Tom is wonderfully, thoughtlessly, content. He hums happily and tunelessly to himself.

Then suddenly he stiffens. His father is climbing up the steep ground at the back of the barn and making for the doorway. This in itself is not startling, rather it is the way he is moving, crouched, as though stalking something. Tom lets the hand holding his knife drop down beside him. He watches in frank amazement. He sees his father pause at the doorway then peer cautiously in, for all the world like a cops-and-robbers film. Has his dad gone nuts or is there some wild animal in there – a mink perhaps? A mink is the only fierce creature Tom can think of likely to be in the barns. Next moment his father slides round the side of the doorway into the loft and vanishes from sight.

Tom knows he's running the risk of discovery, but his curiosity wins out. Leaving his knife and stick he runs down

the side of the hill, flattening himself up against the building as his father has previously done. Tom's heart is
pounding as he listens. He imagines his father about to kill
something, with what he is not quite sure. He's less worried
about being found now, for his dad has no idea of time and
will think he's come back off the bus. Then, to his greater
amazement, Tom hears the sound of Tamsin's and his
father's voices – not loud and normal, but low, almost as if
they're sharing a secret. Tom's eyes grow wider as he tries
to make sense of it. They must be looking at something
they've never seen before, to be talking like that. Shall he
go in? He takes a deep breath. His curiosity overcomes his
fear of detection and, copying his father, he slides round
the doorway.

For a few seconds his eyes don't acclimatize, and the
barn is dark as dark. Then Tom sees, quite close to the
opening on the yard side, his father kneeling above
Tamsin, who is lying on her back across the bales. Tom
stands, uncomprehending. Then a peculiar feeling of fear
and disgust rises up in him. He closes his eyes; he doesn't
want to see. Hardly knowing what he is doing, he silently
slips out of the barn by the way he has come. For a few
seconds he stands trembling, then he scrambles back up the
hill to the side of the barn, so that no one can see him
should they look out. Once in the coppice, he flings himself
on his stomach, grasps handfuls of pine needles, and rubs
his face in the moist, sandy earth as if treating it with
unnatural roughness will obliterate what his eyes have
seen.

'Thank you ever so much.' Dora climbs out of the pick-up
with difficulty, lifting her heavy bags.

'Are you sure you won't let me drive you down your
lane?' John Barnett leans across to shut the door.

Dora's lips are firmly set. She's put him to enough
trouble already; she can manage perfectly well, thank you.
She sets off walking as straight as possible till he has driven
out of sight round the corner. Dora is proud. She doesn't

want people like the Barnetts to know most of the slates are off the barn since the last gale, nor to see the burial mounds of rusting machinery and derelict cars. She used to go for Ben about his cars at one time, but has long since given up the fruitless task. Roughly every six months, usually on a Sunday after chapel, he'd go out to the local scrap merchant and bring home a defunct car, towed it home sometimes. It was always the same story; he was going to do it up. But weeks, months, years later, they were all still at the side of the lane, untouched. Ron put his foot down at last, when there was no more space, but not before Ben collected himself a dozen scrap cars. Dora doesn't mind so much about other people like herself, but the Barnetts are a different matter. Their children go away to boarding school. Mr Barnett employs someone to work the farm for him. Mrs Barnett's very good mind, she's done a lot for the village; but then she's in a position to, isn't she? Edith knows them a lot better than Dora because she goes along twice a week to clean up for Mrs Barnett. She enjoys it, it gets her out, she says. Dora thinks it's because Edith's nosy and likes poking around the houses of the well-to-do, seeing what they've got. After Edith's first morning she came along the same afternoon to see Dora.

'Oh my,' She said. 'You should see! It's a beautiful place. I know it well because I used to do for Miss Bramley back before I came out here with Arthur. But haven't they changed it! All the dark floors gone golden – polyurethane, she says it is. And all the staircase painted white. They made the old stable into a downstairs cloakroom – green toilet, green wash-basin, green tiles, ever so smart. All the walls painted white or chocolate. To be honest with you, I don't like the chocolate, nor do I like those horrible pictures they've got everywhere. Modern paintings. I can't see nothing to them myself.'

Dora jerks out of her recollections. She thought she heard someone call. She is only about seventy-five yards from the yard and buildings. The rusting machinery she prefers the Barnetts not to see lines the lane on either side in brambled humps. Old birds' nests from last year show themselves clearly set in the brambled arches. Dora stops to listen: nothing. She quickens her pace in spite of her aching arms. Tom won't be home yet so it can't be Tom. She herself is earlier than expected owing to the lift. A moment later she definitely hears voices from the hay loft ahead and above. She rounds the corner into the yard.

'Don't, don't, *don't*.' Tamsin's voice is clear enough now.

'Tamsin?' Dora hurries forward beneath the open door above her.

'Tamsin?'

Silence. Absolute.

Then a rustle of hay and the murmur of a low voice. Dora is startled. Her mind flies back to tea with Edith. Surely it can't be that Sanders boy up there with her?

'Tamsin,' Dora calls more sharply. 'Come and speak to me.'

A further rustle and sounds of movement above. Then Tamsin appears in the open doorway.

'What are you doing up there? Who's with you?'

'Dad.'

Dora sighs with relief. So it isn't that boy. She screws up her eyes to see the better.

'What was you shouting about?'

Tamsin looks over her shoulder, then back down at Dora. 'He rolled a hay-bale down on me,' she says.

'What are you doing up there?' Dora is still puzzled.

'Giving Dad a hand.'

'Well, come down and give me a hand with these stores.' Dora lifts the bags she has lowered on to the cobbles beside her, and makes for the house.

Tamsin walks to the back of the barn, giving her father a wide skirting. Ben stands sullen, resentful.

'Wait a moment, can't you?'

Tamsin stops in the doorway, her hand supporting her, silhouetted black against the sky outside.

'What?'

'You won't go talking?' He's almost pleading. Tamsin looks back at him, hatred and contempt written all over her face. She sees no need to answer. Instead she disappears; the doorway shows only the green hill rising behind, the top of the ridge, and the white sky. Ben blunders to the opening above the yard, throws down two bales, then follows Tamsin out of the back. Who knows what goes on in his poor, frustrated, alcohol-impeded mind? He is despised and mocked by all – except his own children who live in terror of him, his brother who tolerates him, and his sister who adores him. That's life, isn't it. Lucky Ben, to have a sister whose love, to date, seems a good bit stronger than God's. Or is this, perhaps, the root of the trouble?

Rachel's anxiety is mounting. Her boss has rung to confirm he'll be along as usual between five and six this evening. Why hasn't Tamsin come or rung? Joe has cleared off for the day. He's edgy and restless; he finds fault with everything Rachel does. She's quite glad of a breather, a few moments to herself to think about the till. Not that there's any point in thinking, she tells herself as she screws a nozzle on a petrol tank, it's simply a matter of laying her hands on the money and putting it back in. She's already put in the whole of her previous week's wage, apart from the £12 she kept out to keep Joe and herself. And most of that, except for cigarette money, has gone on Joe. Rachel knows she's daft but that's the way she is – it's her way of keeping Joe.

The driver is looking round impatiently out of his window, waiting for her, waving a £5 note. Rachel takes it, goes in and taps out the change on the machine. She looks at herself briefly in the small mirror with pin-ups stuck round it. What she sees isn't comforting. Worry, she decides, is very ageing. She must wash her hair. Clean hair takes several years off your age.

The customer sounds his horn impatiently. He'll remember not to come to this garage again – not that he comes to the South West often; too much rain. They're slow down here too, compared to London. Take this woman, what the hell is she doing now? Rachel has walked out of the door and is absentmindedly approaching the second-in-line. The first driver shouts:

'Over here with my change, luv, I haven't got all bloody day.'

Rachel starts and changes direction. She's still wondering about her face and how to get rid of those small lines low down between the cheek and mouth. She decides to buy that very expensive vitamin E cream just as soon as the money is straightened out. She hands the change through the first car window. The driver looks at her angrily. Slow and stupid as a cow, he thinks. Rachel apologizes. She's used to rude, unpleasant customers. At this moment she catches sight of Tamsin by the bridge, coming into the yard. The first car drives off noisily, the second pulls into position in front of the pumps. Automatically Rachel takes down the hose nozzle, her hand on the lever.

'Four, four-star,' the driver is shouting at her out of the window.

Rachel puts back the three-star pump and takes down the other. Why doesn't Tamsin hurry? Has she got it?

'Two, I only want two.' The driver is getting frantic. He hasn't the cash to pay for more and this silly idiot woman doesn't seem to know what she's doing.

Rachel puts the nozzle in the tank. Tamsin is within earshot now, without Rachel shouting or being overheard.

'Have you got it?'

Tamsin nods. She hesitates.

'Go on in the house, then. I'll be with you in two minutes.'

Tamsin vanishes through the spring door that slams behind her. Rachel goes to take the pay.

'Hot, is it dear?' The driver looks at her pityingly. Surprised, Rachel wipes her arm across her forehead. She finds it wet with sweat.

'Gone a lot milder,' she mumbles, taking the money. Thank God it's exact. She hurries into the office, turning the 'open' sign round to 'closed' on the door, and goes through to the back. Tamsin is on the settee, her legs gawkily stuck out in front of her, toes turned in. She's wearing her pleated school skirt and blazer; she's even got her beret on today. Rachel is brought up short by how young she looks – perhaps it's the uniform. Tamsin only wears it sometimes, and Rachel hasn't seen her in it before.

'Well?' Rachel asks.

Tamsin feels in her blazer pocket and pulls out the bundles of notes, holds them out to Rachel. It is the kind of moment to bring tears to most people's eyes, Tamsin handing Rachel the notes so dearly paid for, but Rachel can't know this. She leaps at them with joy; those worry lines vanish without vitamin E. Rachel flings her arms round Tamsin and kisses her.

'You angel! How did you manage?'

Tamsin tells her, but she doesn't tell all. She thought she would but when it comes to it she can't say it, not even to her mother.

'All in all,' I said, 'I think it might be best if I came up to London with you.'

Mum didn't look as pleased as I thought she would. She sat there in her chair smoking for a bit, then she got up and tapped a fresh fag on the mantel before she lit it.

'I don't know what to say, Tamsin,' she said at last. 'There's your school work. You seemed so keen on it when you first come out here.'

'Yes,' I said.

'So what'll happen about that? You oughter get your 'O's.'

'I know,' I said. 'But I haven't done so well lately.'

'You been coming along here evenings instead of working,' she said. She still seemed unwillingly for me to go with them.

'Please, Mum,' I said. 'I don't want to go on living out the farm.'

'I can see that,' my mother said. She seemed in a real

106

dilemma. She had her elbow resting on the mantel and her forehead in her hand.

'I can go back in school when we get to London,' I said. 'Do my 'O's in the autumn.'

'Yes,' she said, kind of automatic like. I couldn't see there was any further problem.

At last she turned away from the mantel and looked at me. 'It's like this,' she said. 'We won't have much money – only a bit I'll get for my holiday pay when I leave this place plus a bit more. Living's not going to be easy. Joe and I was going to stay with some friends he's got up there, till we can find a place on our own. But having you along with us would complicate things. I don't know that they'd have room for you . . .

I sat while Mum talked on. I was hardly listening because I'd got the message. She didn't want me, that was the long and short of it. First I felt bitter, having got her the money and all that; then I felt sorry for myself and tears came in my eyes. I looked up at her hopefully. I thought it would make a difference if she saw how upset I was.

'. . . So,' she was saying, 'it'd be better if you waited and let us get a place up there for you to come to.'

The thought of years at the farm stretched out ahead of me, grey and misty and wet with mud and Auntie ordering me about. I didn't think I could bear it. Then there was Dad. I didn't dare to think about him. I couldn't go on living there with him. I said as much to my mother.

She looked helplessly at me. 'How would you have managed if I hadn't come along?'

I felt like saying today would never have happened. Dad wouldn't have blackmailed me into getting his way with me. But somehow I couldn't tell her about it, I just couldn't. All I did was repeat, 'I don't like living out the farm with Dad.'

Maybe my mother guessed something, I don't know, because she came forward right close, knelt down in front of me, and said:

'What is it about your father that's so bad?'

I couldn't speak. I thought if I spoke I'd cry.

'Tell me, Tamsin,' she said.

I still couldn't.

'You didn't like him,' I said at last, 'otherwise you wouldn't have left him.'

She got up and walked away when I said that, stood with her back to me. I thought she was angry, and so she was in a way. When she spoke her voice was different, sort of hard and detached.

'You don't know what it was like for me being a stranger among the Bands,' she said. 'Dora hated me from the start. I don't think it was me in particular. I think she'd have resented anyone marrying Ben. She was living there before I came, she regarded it as her place. I was an intruder, a fancy-bit Ben had picked up. I told Ben I'd go back north to my mother if Dora stayed under the same roof.' Mum lit another of her endless fags. 'Three months later she was still there, running the place. I shared Ben's bed and went out drinking with him, evenings. Oh I did what she asked me around the place, I wasn't no dead weight. Then one night, I think it must have been a Saturday, I was up in our room above the kitchen – you know what it's like, you can hear everything that's said up through the plank floor. I heard Ben come in and Dora start up at him. He was tipsy, that was true enough, but she was keeping on at him as though he wasn't a man at all, maybe her own kid, though I wouldn't want to treat a kid like that. Ben wasn't saying much, he never was much of a talker, and I couldn't stand for to hear how she was bullying him, I didn't see she had a right to. So I went down the stairs and pushed open the door. Soon as she saw me she quit talking. I walked into the room, pulled out a chair and sat myself down at the table.

' "Dora," I said, "either you're going or I am. Which is it to be?" It took a bit of courage for me to say that, mind, because I was a lot younger than she was. Age means more when you're young.

'Dora looked at Ben. Ben was scared of her, always had been, her being his elder sister, more or less his mother too, seeing how his mother died when he was four. Then she said, "If Ben asks me, I'll go", daring him, like.

'I sat waiting with the clock ticking away loud, I shan't ever forget it. Then Ben stood up. It was as if he had to stand to get his courage. Even now I think what made him say what he did was being a bit tipsy; not drunk, but just enough to stimulate him, make him set on coming up to me that night, I don't know. Anyway, he stood there, his head up between the beams – he was tall enough – and said:

' "I reckon Rachel's my wife, her's the woman here."

'Dora looked fit to crack. She went up to her room right then, packed herself five suitcases and made Ben drive her to her cousin's the other side of Meridan. And that's where she stayed till I left.'

Mum sat down. It seemed as though she'd finished. I could picture it all, clear as anything, but she still hadn't told me the one thing I wanted to know: why she'd left Dad. From what she said it sounded like they didn't get on bad at all.

So I came out with it again.

'Why did you leave Dad?' I said.

'I was coming to that part,' my mother said. 'Give me time.' Cars were coming in the yard, seeing the closed sign, sounding their horns in anger and driving off.

'Mum,' I said, 'shouldn't I go out and turn the "open" sign round in front of the pumps?'

'Yes,' she said, 'you go and do that.'

When I came back she was in the bathroom washing her hair. She came out in a few minutes and sat down with the drier. It was a proper noisy one, no one could talk with it going, so I switched on the telly.

When her hair was dry she went through in her bedroom and came back with a comb. With her hair straight round her face she looked different. Her face looked white and plain and tired. Strained, I suppose you'd call it. I felt sorry for her then. Her life didn't seem as good as it'd first seemed to me.

But I was at her again, like a fly round fly-paper, I couldn't let it go.

'Why did you leave Dad?'

'I dunno,' she said. 'I don't think I was cut out for that sort of life – going to market once a week, keeping the house and cooking. I cut out chapel straight away; neither Ben nor I went. Ron did sometimes. Another thing, Dora never let go the accounts even though she wasn't living there. She had a share in the place, see, a third of it. It was divided between the three of them by old man Band. That way there's not a one of them can afford to buy the other two out, and in any case they like it. I doubt if any of them could live away from it. Dora was always there in the background, even when she was gone. She came once a week, Sunday between five and six, to see Ben. She made do with Ron if he wasn't around. Talked finance. She never missed a week so far as I know. I didn't care about the financial side of the place, not at first. Then when I found Ben wasn't giving me any money at all except what came out his pocket for a round of drinks down the pub, I got resentful. I'd always been, well, independent I suppose you'd call it, gone out to work even when I was at school, done a bit of night-work even. So being stuck out there on the farm with no means at all except the odd hand-out from Ben wasn't my idea of living at all. I felt sort of . . . half dead. I don't know how to put it . . .'

'Yes,' I said, 'I know just how you mean. That's how it is with me.'

She looked at me. 'You can't know how it was for me because times have changed. It wasn't so easy to get your dole money then – not for someone young, healthy and married like I was, anyways.' She paused. 'Then you were born,' she said.

I could tell she hadn't wanted me, not that I'd ever supposed she had. I'd just come along like most babies did, back along before there was much in the way of family planning and clinics and all that. I got the picture pretty clear now. She'd probably tried to abort me. I imagined her hanging over the bridge and wondering whether to jump into the pool; leaping out of hay lofts; stealing money for gin – all sorts.

'I admit I wasn't over the moon about it,' she said, reading my thoughts. 'But as time went on I resigned myself; most of us do. Towards the end I was longing for you. My own baby, I couldn't wait. I prepared the small room at the end of the landing and bought a wickerwork cot down the market. You were born in April just when the sun was melting the snow on the roof of the house. I was lying there in labour, listening to it avalanche off with a great rush and thump. The ground was thawing too and the wild daffs were coming through. I was happy then . . . for a while. Ben was attentive too; he was pleased as punch you were a girl. He wanted Dora to see you but I wouldn't let her. I thought she'd cast an evil spell on you or something. I couldn't stand that woman.'

She lit another cigarette. I felt guilty sitting listening to Mum saying things about my aunt. She'd been fair to me, mothered me, even though she preferred Tom. I felt bad saying nothing in her defence but I was too keen to hear the rest of what she had to say.

'Time ran on. I had Tom. It was after Tom I began to feel trapped out Ventnor stronger than ever before. And never any money. For food, yes. Enough. And for things about the house. But no spending money. I'd stopped liking it with Ben too. I was too dead scared of more kids. Two was enough for me. Of course that made Ben mad. He started going out by himself drinking instead of me going along with him. It wasn't possible any longer anyhow, with you two. Ron would mind you sometimes but he wasn't much of a hand with kids.'

I said I couldn't remember.

'So, as I said, Ben started drinking on his own and coming home drunk and belligerent, busting the doorcatch if I shut him out our bedroom, till I couldn't take any more of it. I told Ben one night, I said, "If you don't stop your drinking and give me more money for the kids

111

I'm quitting – I mean it." All he said was:
' "Quit quick, if that's what you want."
' "I'd go tonight if it wasn't for the kids," I said. "Go on,"
he said. "Go." Then he started hammering me, laying into
me like a punchball.

'I hated him. I got right up out of my bed and walked
away from that place. I never been back since. Left everything, even you kids, and I cared for you all right. I expect I
must have been a bit funny in the head at the time.'

She stopped, lit another fag. I didn't say anything for fear
she wouldn't go on.

'I found a room in return for housework. When I got
round to writing a letter to Ben asking for both of you to
come down Taverston, I got a letter back in Dora's hand-
writing. It said I wasn't fit to rear you, and she was back and
looking after you both proper. She'd made Ben sign it.'

I could tell by her voice Mum was quite worked up by
thinking about it. She didn't go on, just sat a long while
smoking in silence. I had plenty to think about too. It was
getting dark outside, partly because of the rain clouds. I felt
cold.

'Can I plug in the fire?' I asked.

Ron is whistling as he drives the trailer along. That he's
whistling means he is thinking of other things, that he's
happy even. The day is still and mild, the sun shines
brightly down on the old red bonnet of the tractor; the
diesel fumes shunt up thinly against the hedge-sparrow
egg-blue of the sky. Ron whistles. He looks up at the dark
ridge of moor on his left and down over the fields to the
stream on his right. Suddenly his whistling stops. He puts
on the brakes. What is that grey-white shape against the
hedge on the left? Can it be his missing black-face sheep?
He abandons the tractor in the lane, climbs the gate and
approaches the hedge. As he draws closer the shape
lunges. Ron is relieved: not dead; lucky he saw it. He pulls
out his knife, catches the lunging sheep, and cuts away the
brambles that have enmeshed it more effectively than a

barbed-wire entanglement. Once freed, he lets it go. It scampers off dizzily, first in one direction, then, changing its mind, in another. Brambles still trail from its long shaggy fleece. The hedge beside Ron is covered with wool like old man's beard. He reckons the sheep must have been there a couple of days. He closes his knife and walks back to his tractor. As he does so he hears a car engine humming along the road on the other side of the valley. He looks to see if he recognizes it. At first he can't see it winding along the lane between the high banks, but then he catches sight of it passing behind a gateway, and again where the bank is low and the thorn on top has died. He doesn't recognize it, yet it seems to him he has seen it before though he can't think where. It's an old black car. Ron scratches his head. He should know it. He looks back at the road. To his surprise the car stops at the top of Ventnor lane, engine still turning over. The sun from the south-east slides from behind a clump of trees; it shines on Ron's glasses, dazzles him. He takes off the glasses, and wipes them on a bit of rag in his pocket as though he has not realized it is the brilliance of the sun that stops him seeing. When he looks back at the road, the black car has moved on, now passing along a section of road behind a tumbledown wall. Ron has a clear view of it but still cannot place it. He is too far away to see the driver.

He loses interest and climbs into the tractor. He drives on to the end of the lane, where, in pools of slimy, sucking mud, the bullocks stagger around waiting for the hay on the back of the tractor. Whistling again, Ron pushes open the gate, ploughs through the mud to drier ground, and jumps down leaving the tractor just edging its way forward. He climbs on the link box at the back, slashes the baler cord, and hurls the hay out to the cattle, who follow, grabbing a mouthful, pushing off each other, and generally hastening in the hay wake of the tractor. As he automatically performs his task Ron casts his expert stockman's eye over his herd. They are looking well, for the time of year. He climbs off the link box, gets back on the tractor and stops it. He sits contentedly watching his cows and calves, picking out at this early stage the ones he will keep to replace his herd, and the ones he will sell in the suckled-calf sales.

High above him two larks soar and sing. Spring. Ron's feeling of well-being increases. His dog, who he has let out and forgotten about, now reappears shame-faced. She has been off rabbiting. When she sees she is not in trouble, she races forward and bounds up at him joyously. He curses her amicably and she cowers. Ordering her away, he turns the key of the tractor. He goes back by the way he has come, still whistling.

'Tamsy?' Joe's voice is soft and tender as he bends over the rounded, relaxed shape of Tamsin in the seat beside him.

She stirs sleepily, turns her unsullied cherry lips towards him. He bends over and kisses them gently.

'Oh, Joe,' Tamsin breathes, stretching her downy arms up round Joe's neck and drawing his head back to her mouth.

'It's late.'

Tamsin breaks off in the middle of a kiss. 'Late? What time is it?'

'Nearly eight.'

Tamsin sits up. She is stiff now that she moves; her back aches. She feels bruised. She can see nothing, for the windows of the car are misted up.

'What am I to say?' she murmurs in alarm. 'I meant to get in while it was still dark.'

'Say you missed the last bus, had to wait for a lift this morning.'

Tamsin is looking for her shoes. She can't think clearly, she is aware trouble is coming.

Joe gets out. He relieves himself behind a clump of gorse and takes stock of his surroundings. Moor stretches away on either side, black and brown and bleak as becomes the time of year. A few ponies are grazing up on the side of the tor-capped hill in front of him; nearer the car are some hill sheep. Joe fastens his zip and returns to Tamsin, who is doing her hair in the mirror. She has wiped the condensation off her window. She looks panicky.

'Quick, Joe,' she says. 'I have to get back. If I'm not in school today they'll start asking questions.'

'They'll see you when you go back to the farm, won't they?' asks Joe. 'Why don't you go straight to school?'

Tamsin's face brightens. 'OK,' she says. 'Drop me at the top of the lane, will you, and I won't go down to the farm at all. Tom'll see me but I can fix him.'

So Joe drives and Tamsin lies back in the seat beside him so no one they pass will have seen two in the car. She looks up at the white sky and the branches of trees that wave across the road. She feels contented all over her body; every inch of her feels soft and pliable and full of love. She turns her head sideways and looks at Joe. She adores him, she is in love.

But now another feeling starts to emerge, the feeling of guilt. What about her mother? Tamsin can't bear to think. She shuts her eyes as though shutting out her thoughts.

'Joe,' she asks finally, 'are you going to London with Mum?'

'I'm going to London,' he says, shortly.

'And leaving her?' Tamsin sounds shocked. Deceiving doesn't seem as final as leaving.

'It's finished,' Joe says, with all the callousness of youth.

They drive in silence while Tamsin indulges in suffering, for herself and for her mother. She pictures them weeping in each other's arms; her bravely comforting her mother without admitting that she too loves Joe – he is the great passion she has been waiting for and now found.

She glances at his profile again and slips a hand delicately on to his jeaned thigh. He covers the small hand with his large one and drives along one-handed. What actually concerns him is getting rid of Tamsin as quickly as possible now night is passed. If the police pick him up again in this same car he'll have had his chips, he knows that. He lets go Tamsin's hand to change gear. They slip across the crossroads. Another half-mile and he can drop Tamsin and go back on the other road.

Tamsin looks down at her laddered tights. They do look rather awful. Oh well, she'll be able to show it to Karen as proof. She'll tell Karen everything except who it was with. Pleasure suffuses Tamsin at the thought of telling all to Karen. Well, almost all.

'Get ready,' Joe says brusquely. Tamsin looks at him anxiously, but does as he says. She leans over the back seat for her satchel. As she does so a horrid thought comes into her head. The £50: will her aunt have missed it? She reassures herself with the thought today is Friday. Her mother will get paid, pay her back and she will pay back her aunt. In fact she will greet her aunt this evening holding the returned cash. Or if her aunt hasn't found it missing, she will unobtrusively slip it back in the desk.

The car stops.

''Bye, Joe.' Tamsin leans her face across to be kissed.

Joe supplies a quick one. Why can't the silly girl stop fooling and get out?

'Joe?'

'What?'

'Kiss me just once. Properly.' Her moist lips are within inches of his. He kisses her in desperation. Perhaps now she'll go.

'You don't want the coppers to get me again, do you?'

Tamsin hurriedly gets out. She wants to ask when she'll see him again but daren't. The car drives off. She waves at its humped back swaying round the corner, then reassesses her own situation. Tom should come up the lane in ten minutes; the school bus should come along in fifteen, roughly. She could try to get down to the farm without being seen but it is really too risky. By now her aunt has almost certainly discovered she didn't come back last night. It'll be best if she thinks she spent the night at Denise's. Tamsin sits down patiently. She feels very hungry, but that'll have to wait. She's really, been incredibly lucky. So far everything's worked out, more or less. How much longer can her luck hold? she wonders. Her father's face flashes in front of her in close-up. She winces and pushes the image from her conscious mind.

From her right she hears someone coming up the lane. She shrinks back against the bank under the holly. God let it be Tom, she murmurs. God let it be Tom. She cranes her head forward an inch or two and looks. It is Tom, dilly-dallying and whirling his satchel round and round. He's got his catapult for shooting at harmless little birds he never hits. Cruel Tom, it's much worse to torture poor little creatures than great big humans the same size as you are. Isn't it?

Rachel is still waiting for her boss. It's late. Rachel has been out all afternoon, trying for another saleswoman job. It's what she'd like as it gives her the loan of a car and the chance of getting out and about, covering quite long distances, meeting people. But of course if she goes to London with Joe . . . Rachel starts to chew her fingers. She'd like to, oh yes she'd like to, but somehow she can't quite imagine it. Though she's nuts about Joe she's stopped kidding herself for some time that he feels the same way about her. Well, she knows he doesn't, that's all there is to it. Still, he might take her with him for the money. Rachel faces the bleak situation squarely. What else is there for her to do? She knows there's others, though not who. Diane is one, because the woman in the chemist told her, let it out by mistake. Or perhaps it wasn't by mistake. Then there's Tamsin. She knows Joe's been eyeing her but she doesn't imagine it's gone very far – yet. What she doesn't know is that Joe waylaid Tamsin on her way up to the bus stop last night and gave her a lift in the usual borrowed car. She doesn't think Joe'd be fool enough to drive that car again after the coppers have had him. She's forgotten what a man'll do to get a woman before he's had her. Her mind reverts back to money. Joe'll never pay his fine; she'll have to. Why doesn't her boss come? At least she'll have this week's pay *and* can give in her notice *and* can ask for her two weeks' holiday pay. Then, for a week or so, she'll be rich. Beyond that Rachel doesn't care to think. She's burning her boats already. London or the selling job, it will have to be one or the other because she's not prepared to fool about with the dole, and that's for sure.

A car purrs quietly into the yard. She jumps up, looks out the window. Her boss switches off the engine and sits in his slighty battered and out-of-date but still smooth Jag. Rachel goes joyfully out to meet him. He follows her into the office. She invites him through for a cup of tea or coffee. He chooses coffee. Rachel plugs in the kettle, stands with one hand on the handle talking of this and that. Alvin Harris has had a hard week, been busy, is exhausted. Rachel can't help thinking him the most unattractive man she's ever seen: white thin face, pale thin hair scattered over the pale white scalp, pale eyebrows. His face seems to culminate in his mouth, nose and chin. Ratty, she thinks, and shudders a little. She's glad she's giving in her notice despite losing this place.

Alvin is talking in a pale flat voice. Rachel hands him coffee, takes her own and sits opposite him with her cup in a saucer resting on her knees. She's not used to a saucer. She's simply using one because of him.

Fifteen minutes later he is still talking when Joe walks in. Rachel stands quickly. What is Joe thinking of? He knows her boss doesn't know about him. Rachel makes a face at Joe indicating to him to go, but Joe doesn't seem to notice. He sits himself down on the settee next to Alvin, who edges into the corner. Has Joe been drinking? Rachel wonders. She thinks of all the times she's waited and longed for him and he hasn't come. Now it's obvious he's not going. She goes to make him a cup of tea; it gives her time to think. In the kitchen she decides she'd better introduce them, so she goes back.

'This is Mr Harris, Joe. Joe is a friend of my daughter's, he's very good with machines. Gives a hand in the garage sometimes.' Rachel feels she has been inspired. The words just came, it seemed. She returns to the teabag feeling

118

more relaxed, drops it in the sink as Joe likes it weak, and returns with the cup and saucer, which Joe immediately spills. Was it on purpose? She could kill him. She goes out again to get a cloth. When she returns Joe and Alvin are discussing Jag engines. She wipes up, then sits listening. Will they never stop? Will Joe never clear out so she can tell her boss she's leaving? It's not the kind of thing you can do easily with someone else listening. She collects the empty cups, treading on purpose on Joe's foot and looking at him meaningfully. Joe doesn't seem to notice her look. He simply withdraws his foot.

An hour later Alvin Harris leaves. As he goes he hands Rachel her pay packet. She opens her mouth to tell him she's going but all she says is 'thanks' and takes it. The spring door shuts. She hasn't even asked for her holiday pay. She feels desperate and fatalistic. Joe has prevented her. It has all been his fault.

Joe says it's nothing to do with him; he hasn't prevented her doing or saying anything. If she'd decided to give in her notice she should have done so.

'You don't understand,' says Rachel helplessly. 'It's difficult enough when you've worked for someone three years and they're dependent on you. But with a third person hanging around, listening, it's downright impossible.'

'There's always next week,' says Joe complacently.

'What about London?' Rachel asks.

'What about it?'

They were supposed to have gone at the end of next week, weren't they? Joe is not sure, his plans are vague. Rachel looks at him curiously. A week ago he was dead set on it.

'But we *are* going, aren't we?' she demands, anxious. If she gives up everything here and they don't go, she'll be in a pickle.

'Us'll go soon as we're ready,' says Joe, oddly placid. Rachel can't understand it, but as she's actually got Joe who's come for the night, she lets it pass. She might as well make the most of the present, 'gather ye rosebuds while ye may' and all that. Soon Rachel and her rosebud have slipped beneath the quilt. Joe is happy to lie on his back while Rachel makes love to him. He's got a lot of planning to do. Finally he rolls over on top of Rachel and does what is expected of him.

'You're so lucky, Tammy.'

'Yes,' I said, 'I know I am' – in some ways, I thought, but not in others. Supposing I'd told Karen the lot, about the money, and getting it with Dad there, and all that. Would she still have thought me lucky?

'Tell me what he looks like again.'

'Tall,' I said, 'wavy hair, not too short, blue eyes with long black lashes, better'n any girl's—' I stopped.

'Go on,' she said.

'His body's gorgeous,' I said. 'Hard and brown. Muscles but not bulgy ones. He's got nice hands too. Strong and ever so sensitive.' I leant forward and whispered the next bit.

Karen's eyes were popping out.

'With his tongue?' she asked.

'Course,' I said casual, as though masses of people had done it before. 'How else?'

She was silent.

'What does it feel like,' she said at last, 'when he does it proper? Is it the most wonderful thing that's ever happened in your life – like the mags say?'

'It's better'n what they say,' I said. 'Different.'

'How different?'

I couldn't say. I felt that what I'd had with Joe was special, that no one else had ever had it quite the same.

'After,' I said, 'you feel as though you've had all there is in life. You feel if you died right then it wouldn't matter, you'd be happy.'

'What about having a baby?' said Karen. 'That must be marvellous too.'

'Yes,' I said, doubtfully. 'I suppose there's that.' God,

don't let me be pregnant, I murmured under my breath.

Then the bell went and we had to go into lessons. I sat right at the back to keep out of sight. I hadn't done any proper homework for days. I dreaded being picked on. I tried hard to concentrate but I couldn't. Too much was going on in my head. There was Joe and me. Every time I thought of that a thrill went through me that left me feeling almost faint; my knees felt weak. I kept thinking of his hand on my breast. Sometimes I could recreate it almost as though it was happening, then it would vanish and I couldn't get the feeling back. Instead would come all the black things, the things I dreaded: fear over my aunt missing the money, guilt over Mum, disgust and shame over what I'd let Dad do to get the money. I couldn't bear to think of the last. I shut it out of my head. I'd never tell anyone about that, never . . .

The bell went and I'd only heard the first sentence of the lesson. I kept well behind Karen till Miss Shanklin had gone, then took my satchel and ran for the bus. I only just made it. I went up on the top deck.

Half an hour later I went through the swing door of the garage into the back.

Silence. No sign of anyone.

One thing that struck me as odd was the till was open. In the drawers were a few coins, nothing else. I shut it, then changed my mind and opened it again. I didn't want anyone accusing me of interfering with the till. I went out, walked round the yard, through the garage, and out the back into the yard of used cars and ones waiting to be seen to. I called: no answer. She must be down the shops. It did seem odd, though, the garage completely abandoned, just like that. I'd never known them leave it before, not without someone around.

I sauntered back across the yard and stood reading the ads Mum put up in the windows for 5p a week. Rooms to let and job ads mainly, though this time there was some puppies and a Belling cooker. Then I heard someone coming. I turned round and there was a copper coming this side of the bridge. My heart turned over and did something. I'd been reared to be scared of coppers and I was. It was no good clearing out. He'd seen me. I just stood reading the ads as though I hadn't seen him, and watching him coming up behind me by the reflection in the window. When I thought he was close enough, I turned round. I thought it wouldn't seem natural if I didn't.

'Were you waiting for someone?' he asked.

We eyed each other.

'I was looking for my mother,' I said. He looked interested. I knew I'd said the wrong thing but what else could I say?

'You're Mrs Band's . . . daughter?'

'Yes.' I wondered how he knew.

He cleared his throat. 'I'm afraid there's been a spot of trouble out here,' he said. 'I'd like it if you'd come down the station with me. Your mother's there.'

My heart went funny again. I thought of the empty till. She'd never be that crazy: I couldn't understand it. Perhaps someone had broken in.

'OK,' I said, kind of jaunty. I didn't want him to know I was in a dead panic. We walked down the street together on opposite sides. I didn't want to be seen by anyone with a copper.

The station was up a bit with a wide-open park in front of it. I was closer to him as we went up the steps, I had to be. Inside I'd expected to see Mum but there was no sign of her. He told me to sit on a bench at the side while he went through a door at the end. I felt completely blank, blank and empty as the inside of that ugly room painted pale green. A photo of the Cornish riviera was stuck up over the electric fire which wasn't on. I got to thinking where the Cornish riviera could be.

Then the office door (I suppose it was to the office) opened, and Mum came out. She looked all in. I didn't have to look long to see that. I wanted to talk to her but they beckoned me in before I could. Anyway I knew she wouldn't want to say anything with the coppers listening.

There were two of them now, the one who'd brought me in and another behind the desk.

'Mum?' I said as she passed, but she hardly seemed to recognize me. She went straight out the doors and off. At least they're not putting her inside, I thought, so it must be someone broken in and done it. I went into the office.

The one behind the desk – the inspector, I suppose – did all the talking. He told me to sit.

'You are Tamsin Band, Mrs Band's daughter. Is that correct?'

'Yes,' I said. He wrote it down.

'You live with your mother?'

'No,' I said.

He looked up at me inquiringly. 'I live out the farm,' I said. 'With Dad and my aunt and uncle, at Ventnor.'

He took all the details, names and addresses, and wrote them down.

'You're still at school, I take it?' He eyed me again. I'd still got my uniform on from the day before. I hadn't been home so I couldn't change out of it.

I didn't reply because it was obvious.

'Could you kindly answer when I speak to you, young woman?' he said.

He took the name and address of my school. I yawned. I couldn't help it. It all seemed pointless. Why didn't he ask me what he wanted to know and let me go after Mum?

Then he did say something that made me sit up. 'Are you friendly with a Joe Sanders?'

I froze. I didn't know what to answer.

'I know him,' I said.

He was writing down everything. It made me nervous, careful.

'How long have you known him?' So it went on, till it came to the question I knew they were bound to ask: was he living out the garage with Mum?

I lied then because I guessed Mum would have lied too. 'No,' I said. 'He just goes out the garage to give her a hand with the pumps some days.'

Did he get paid? I said I didn't know whether he did or not, I thought it was more for something to do as he was out of work.

After that I thought they'd finished with me. The inspector sat back, and I shifted on my chair and picked up my satchel ready to stand.

'Were you with Joe Sanders in a borrowed car last night?'

I shook my head. I didn't have time to think.

'No,' I said.

He wrote it down, then looked at me over his glasses. 'You are telling the truth?' he asked.

'Yes,' I said.

'Good,' he said, and closed his book. 'That'll be all, thank you.'

I felt sick as I stood up. As I went I was on the point of turning back and telling him it was lies. It wasn't them I minded knowing, it was the thought of it getting back to Mum. And my aunt and Dad. Mum above all. Whatever would she think of me?

I went out of the station and the door closed behind me. It seemed the whole of my life had changed during the half-hour I'd been in there. I wondered how much she knew already, how much they'd told her. It wasn't till I was halfway back up the road to the garage that I realized I'd never even asked them why they were questioning me in the first place. Was it the borrowed car? Where was Joe? Was it because they'd got Joe in they were questioning Mum?

'Dad, were you out Kember the other night?'

Ben looks across the table at Tom, who is looking at him earnestly.

'Dunno,' he says. 'I might'a been, and then I might not.' He regards Tom with suspicion. 'What do you want to know for?'

Dora, over in the corner, her account book open on her lap, pauses in her adding. She too looks at Tom.

'Nothing,' says Tom.

Ben glowers at him. 'Then don't do it,' he says. 'Don't go asking questions for nothing.'

'Haven't you got any homework, Tom?' Dora asks. Then, before he can answer, 'Tamsin's in trouble, Ben, you don't need to go for Tom. Ringing me up at eight this morning to say she been and spent the night with her mother. I didn't get no sleep for worrying about her.'

Ben says nothing. He's on tricky ground as regards Tamsin. He grunts.

'It's for you to be strict with her,' says Dora. 'She takes more notice of you than what she would of me.'

Ben shuts his eyes. Tom slips away upstairs, gets out his needle on the end of the thread and holds it over his map fastened to the marble top of the washstand with blue-tac.

He shuts his eyes and repeats to himself, 'Where was Tamsin last night, where was Tamsin last night?' Soon the needle miraculously slows its waving and starts to rotate in small circles. Tom unfastens his eyes and looks down. The needle isn't over Asherford, it's over the moor. Tom's eyes grow big with excitement, he'll try it again. He repeats his incantation. When he next opens his eyes the needle is circling over a different place. Tom gets up, disappointed. Something is wrong. He walks to the window and sees a magpie. Dashing down the stairs he bursts into the kitchen in search of his catapult. There he's brought up short. His aunt looks as though she's seen a ghost, and even his dad is taking notice. Tom forgets the magpie. He wants to know what's up.

'Count it for yourself,' his aunt is saying, pushing two bundles of notes in elastic bands in front of Ben. She sees Tom. 'Here, you count 'em with your dad. See if you don't make it £50 short.'

So Ben and Tom pull up chairs to the table and laboriously count. Then again. Ben sits back.

'Dora's right. £50 short.'

Silence except for the clock's ticking. They hear Ron coming back on the tractor.

125

'Fifty pounds short,' says Dora as his head comes in the door.

Ron blinks, takes off his cap and scratches his head; takes off his boots and goes to wash his hands.

'What are we going to do?' Dora is in a panic.

Ron dries his hands. They push all the money towards him. He counts, then reaches for Dora's cash-book, checks the items.

'Fifty pounds short,' he pronounces at last.

Ben thinks back to Tamsin in the office. His mind travels from the office to the hay loft. He stirs uncomfortably, recrosses his feet. It's not for him to say, that's certain. Let them find out for themselves.

'Looks like it's gone,' he says.

Dora is enraged. Tom slithers back into the corner in anticipation and alarm. This is exciting. Perhaps he can find the money with his needle.

'You could've put it someplace else,' Ron says, gazing hopefully at Dora.

'No, I couldn't.' Dora is strident. 'There's nowhere else I ever put the money save in that drawer. That's the place it's been kept the last twenty years, ever since I done the accounting.'

Ron and Ben can't think back to before Dora did the accounting. They wisely remain silent, as anything they say is likely to be wrong. Silence, in fact, proves wrong too.

'Can't you say something?' Dora demands. For some reason, unfathomable to them, she looks expectant.

Silence.

'Very well, then. I'll say it.' Dora quivers. 'Tamsin must have took it.'

Ron looks distressed. 'You ain't got a right to say that, Dora. Why should it be the girl?'

'Rachel's behind it,' Dora says, restoring the two bundles to the cash-box. 'You see if I'm not right.'

Ben takes a silent delight in withholding information from Dora. Ron suspects it is Ben, after pub money. The kitchen feels hot and airless to him. He would rather be outside in the fields where the air is clean. Tom shuffles his feet; they remember he is there.

'You don't know nothing about it, do you Tom?' Dora penetrates him with a look like she tests her cakes with a skewer. Tom edges towards the stair door.

'Course I don't,' he says, looking at her with large resentful eyes. Her heart softens. Tom's a good boy, a lot like Ben was at the same age. She won't let him go the same way Ben has, not if she can help it. Dora sets her lips firmly.

'There's nothing to be done then,' she says, 'till Tamsin comes back.'

Tom slides inconspicuously through the door and up the stairs. Ron remembers something needs doing outside and gets back in his boots. Ben rubs the side of his nose. He too waits for Tamsin, her footsteps approaching the back door, the latch going up – her standing there in her pleated skirt and stockings, tights or whatever. She's taken to wearing them recently instead of socks and it's made a difference, though he can't exactly say what the difference is. A dark dread he can't name steals over him. Supposing Tamsin's taken the money and gone because of him? Will he wait indefinitely, never hear her returning steps, never see the latch pulled up by the string and know it is only the wood of the door that separates him from her, and that in a further moment, she will be standing in front of him holding her books?

So he sits waiting for his daughter. Right and wrong don't come into Ben's head. He has never thought in those terms, only in terms of what he wants, what his instincts, his inclinations urge him towards. He clings to his urge for Tamsin like ivy round a sapling tree. She gives him life. It never occurs to him that he will destroy her. He waits. And in time Tamsin comes.

Rachel has got the television on. She watches it without taking in the picture or hearing the words. She has turned it on because she cannot sit alone in the familiar room that now seems like a cage, a trap. An upheaval has taken place since four p.m. today that she can't assimilate. She goes back over it again and again in her mind. It's a terrible pain she can't assuage, can't understand. Like someone watching a film she sees herself come into the office and find the till drawer pulled wide, the day's takings – quite considerable – gone. Also the £50 of her own pay she has put in the till for safety till Tamsin comes to claim it: about £120 in all. She sees the empty drawer again in her mind and feels physically sick. It stands for so much. She can't pay back Tamsin, that's for certain: but worse, far worse, Rachel is convinced it is Joe who has taken the money and gone – left her, left Rachel, who was willing to put her last drop of life (well anyway, of sex) into Joe. When Rachel had fully taken in that the money had gone, was stolen, she had looked on the back of the door in her pocket where she kept the till key and had found it missing. She had known then it could only be Joe. Joe was the only person with a key to her room, which she locked when she went out. Joe was the only person who knew where she kept the till key.

In a blind rage of hate against Joe and fear for herself, Rachel went first to Joe's friend in Asherford. No one was there, nothing was locked. She went in, up the stairs and into the wide-open room on her left: Joe's room. Empty, except for a discarded pair of jeans that she recognized, some old cardboard boxes, and a couple of blankets heaped on the bed. She picked up the jeans. She had some idea in her head that Joe must leave no traces. She took them downstairs with her, lifted the lid of the dustbin and pushed them down beneath a bag of litter. If anyone does find them, they won't know they're Joe's, she reasoned. Then she made her way towards the police station; quickly at first, then as she neared it, slower and slower. Two forces were at work in Rachel. One: she hoped they would catch Joe, bring him back, prevent him going off with whoever he'd gone off with, because she's sure it's someone; two: she was betraying Joe to the police, playing Judas.

So instead of going straight through the jaw-like swing doors, Rachel hung round outside, while a war raged within her. She was on the point of going back to the garage, saying nothing and waiting till her boss found out the next week. (Joe may even have calculated on this, a week's grace from Rachel. And Rachel might have done it if it hadn't been for Tamsin.) Then a police car drew up behind her in the car park and the local copper got out. Rachel was trapped. She stood awkwardly waiting while he came up the steps.

'What can I do for you?'

Rachel heard herself say, 'There's been a theft out the garage.'

The constable pushed open one of the doors, which pulled both of them through with the suction of a weir. Rachel felt she was drowning. She was about to betray the man she loved more than herself, her life.

Inside she made her report. She simply described how she found the till empty and the money gone. She allowed them to think she had carelessly left the key in the till. That way, she told herself, it could be anyone, not necessarily Joe. They asked her if she was living on her own. Yes, she said. They told her to go back to the garage until she heard anything further.

Rachel went. She served customers in a trance of suffering. At four p.m. they sent for her. Rachel didn't know what she was in for; this time she was grilled. Her pathetic private life was laid bare for all to see. Only details were left for her to conceal from the police. They knew all about Joe, and Tamsin. She was very surprised they knew about Tamsin, but news travels fast in Asherford.

When eventually she left the sergeant's office like a first-timer forced to strip in a Soho club, she was met by the vacant, innocent eyes of Tamsin in the waiting room. Terrified of breaking down, Rachel hurried past her into the street. She gulped cold, clean air, and automatically made her way back to the garage, to sit as now . . . except that since then she has switched on the telly, and taken pills to prevent the pain over her right eye. She imagines everything is caused by the quick-freeze in which she has placed her heart.

Ron walks up the field carrying a rope. Ben follows twenty yards behind. Tom follows Ben. Dora stands at the bottom looking over the gate. A heifer is calving and all is not as it ought to be. Two feet stick out of the cow's rump above a trailing string of slime; she walks round restlessly, contracts, stares at the oncomers with panicky eyes.

Ron stops, takes his fag out and stamps it in the ground, surveys the project. Ben, puffing, comes up alongside him. There is no need to speak, the brothers are lifelong partners in this game. Ron coils the rope, advances. Ben likewise moves in beside the heifer who is driven inexorably into a patch of scrub in the field's top corner. When she can go no further she halts and contracts. Ron takes his chance, slips a loop of rope round the two protruding feet and draws it tight. He backs away on the end of the rope as the heifer heaves forward. Ben and Tom catch the trailing length of rope behind Ron. They pull. She stops. They ease up – she contracts – they heave. The legs come a little way towards them. Ron leaves the rope and goes in close, feels the position of the head. He goes back, joins the others. She contracts.

'Now,' he says.

All three lie back on the rope and heave. Suddenly the head slips out, covered in mucus, eyes shut. A further contraction.

'And again.'

They pull with all their strength. The rest of the black, shiny body slips out on to the ground. The heifer lunges forward, stands shuddering. Ron goes forward, kneels beside the calf, pulls out the tongue, blows into its lungs. Ben and Tom join him. The heifer lows, anxious, uncertain; turns round.

'It's breathing.' Ron can't conceal the joy in his voice. He rubs its back, pulls its ears; then stands and moves back. The three of them stand watching while the mother moves

130

in, sniffs, and starts rhythmically licking the dark wet calf.

Ron turns away, wipes his hands. He'll come back presently, make sure the calf is up. Ben pushes his cap to the back of his head. Perhaps, he thinks, if Ron weren't so good at everything, he'd do more, take over a bit. But as long as Ron is around . . . Ben doesn't pursue the thought. He walks back down the field. Tom runs.

'What is it?' Dora ask over the gate.

'Heifer calf,' says Ron.

They walk in silence with their separate thoughts back along the lane.

'What now?' I said. 'What am I going to do?'

My mother stared at me with a sort of vacant look. She wasn't seeing me, I knew that. Question was, was she even hearing?

'Mum?' I said.

With an effort she seemed to concentrate on me, what I was saying.

'You'll have to go back to the farm,' she said, a bit distant. 'They'll turn me out of this place. It's no good your staying down here.'

'But the money,' I said. 'If I don't get it back soon, Dora'll find out for sure.' In my mind I pictured my aunt sat over the table with her accounts. I felt desperate. I felt sorry for Mum too. I wondered if she was going to go nuts, but at least she didn't have the Bands to face up to.

'Joe's rotten,' I said out loud. 'Mean as they come.'

Mum said nothing. She went on staring at the electric fire that wasn't on. She's better than me, I thought, she isn't going to blame Joe for a thing. Whereas I could kill him – I would if I could find him.

She seemed to read my thoughts.

'Don't tell them about Joe, will you?' she said.

'No,' I said. I wondered guiltily if I'd said anything already but decided I hadn't. It was them, the coppers, who'd done all the talking.

'So what'll happen?' I asked at last.

'They'll find out where he's gone,' she said. 'They know enough for that. I think they've guessed already. Whether or not they catch him's another matter.'

Silence.

'Do you want them to?' I asked at last.

She didn't answer directly. Then she said, 'I did at first. Now I'm not sure. I don't think I do.'

'But the money,' I repeated like a silly parrot. 'The money I borrowed you?'

She looked at me now, a bit contemptuous, I thought. 'You'll just have to tell them what you've done, won't you?'

So my aunt was right; that was what my mother was like. I stood up. I was quivering a bit, from rage and fear. I put my satchel over my shoulder.

'OK,' I said. 'I'm off. There's no point in me hanging around.' I went over to the door.

'Tamsin?' I looked back at Mum sitting there.

'What?'

'I'm sorry. I never dreamed this would happen, I promise you.'

I fiddled the door handle. I didn't know what to say.

'Will you come back and see me when this is blown over?' she asked.

'Course,' I said. My eyes were blurring. I didn't dare look at her. I went on standing, fiddling the door knob.

Then she was beside me, her arms round me. My shoulders were heaving with sobs, I couldn't help it. She led me back to the settee and I cried and cried while she held me and stroked my hair. Once I'd started I couldn't stop. At one time I looked up and saw her cheeks were wet too.

When I'd quieted a bit, she went and got a toilet roll from the bathroom and I wiped my face and blew my nose. I knew I must look terrible. My face always swells like a lit-up pumpkin when I cry.

'I'd better go,' I said finally, though there was nothing I dreaded more. I knew if I was two nights away they'd come looking for me. I didn't dare send another message through Edith like I had that morning. I thought it'd make them even angrier.

'Yes, go on,' my mother said. 'Tell them just as soon as I can earn it you'll have it back.'

I couldn't somehow believe I'd ever see it back but I didn't say anything. I borrowed a headscarf and tied it round my face like a gran so no one would see I'd been crying, and left. It was dark anyway, as I went up the hill. I couldn't help but think how last time Joe had driven up behind me and picked me up.

The night was clear as anything as I went down the lane. A moon was sinking lower and lower behind the dark ridge of Barrowdown. I thought it was waning though I wasn't sure. I was trying not to think ahead, not to think any more what I was going to say. I'd planned that all the way over in the bus.

My feet made so much noise I walked at the side on the grass. Not for any reason exactly – just I didn't like the noise. It was cold too, ice was on the puddles. I crossed the bridge and up the last bit through the shadowy shapes of Dad's rusted-up cars and into the yard. The lights were on. I knew they'd all be sat round in the kitchen. I didn't know how I was going to face it. I hung around a bit, getting up my courage, but all I got was colder. If I'd had the money I think I'd have run off to London like a looney; run round looking for Joe, work, or something. But I didn't have more than 15p left over from my bus fare, so it was no good dreaming. I pushed open the door, which scraped and screeched along the floor same as usual – no, worse. I think it had got some grit stuck under it.

Coming into the kitchen out of the dark the light seemed bright and glaring; it always does. We don't have lampshades. They're not thought necessary, and we don't have anything but what's necessary at Ventnor. No one said a word as I wiped my feet and walked forward. Then I saw why. Edith was there. That's one thing the Bands'll never do – say a word against any of the family in front of a stranger. I was safe for a bit. I didn't know whether I was pleased or sorry. My aunt said:

'You're late.'

'Yes,' I said. I hung up my coat. Then I walked over and sat by the fire which was lighted. For Edith, I supposed. She must have walked down.

She smiled at me now – artificial. Gossipy old bag! It was her who told my aunt everything, I knew that. I wished she'd go. Now I was in, there seemed no reason to put off what I knew was going to come. I could feel it all round in the air, like before a storm. Everyone was stiller, more polite than usual. Their voices sounded clearer and, at the same time, more distant. The fire was flaming bright; my hands were getting warmer.

I think Edith must have sensed the situation too, thick as she is, because she ended her conversation with my aunt about the wedding she'd been to the day before and stood up.

'I must be getting back,' she said, then went on again for another ten minutes about how to make gloves down the WI. Auntie doesn't go to the WI but she always likes hearing about it. I think she would if she didn't regard it as pleasure sooner than duty. But tonight even she was willing Edith to the door. I could tell by the way she answered 'yes' or 'no', made no effort to ask questions or say anything to set Edith off again. Longing to get at me, I thought. I still didn't know if they'd found out the money was gone, or if the atmosphere I could sense was about staying out all night without telling them. I'd got plenty of excuses for staying out. It was the money that would have me stuck. I waited. I heard the door grate shut and Auntie come back in. I went on warming my hands and looking in the fire, although they were hot and red by now. I had to do something. Ron was into the *Farmer's Weekly* and Dad was rolling a fag.

In fact it was Dad Dora went for.

'Aren't you going to say something, Ben?'

134

Dad looked across at me, and I got that same nasty feeling I always got, even right across the room. My cheeks burned like the fire.

'What you been up to?' he said. 'There's money missing. Your aunt's taken a count.' It was his way of saying he hadn't told.

My heart gave a thump. My hands were shaking so I put them in my lap.

'Fifty pound,' Dora chipped in quick.

Silence. Ron turned a page. Dora looked across at him angrily. 'I think this is your business too, Ron,' she said.

'Your aunt wants to know if you took it.' Dad was blunt enough. I thought he was doing all right, but Dora was incensed.

'It's not me no more'n you or Ron. All of us wants to know if it was you took it, Tamsin.'

'Yes,' I said.

Again it was quiet while the truth sunk in.

'What for?' My aunt couldn't wait for Dad; he was too slow. Now he'd plunged in and broached it, she took over.

'My mother needed £50 to pay back her cash-till,' I said. 'It was only borrowed. She was supposed to give it me back today but someone's pinched it from the till. It'll be all up for her tonight when her boss comes out.'

My aunt's voice dropped almost to a whisper.

'You mean you're involved in a robbery?'

Ron looked up, impatient. 'That's not what she said, Dora. She said it'd been stolen – our money she borrowed for Rachel.' Ron does think straight, I'll give him that.

My aunt sat down as though her legs wouldn't hold her any more.

'You mean we aren't going to see it back?' She'd gone quite white.

'Oh yes, you will,' I said, thinking of Joe, 'if they catch the thief.' I hoped then, for the first time, they wouldn't. I suppose I still loved him, or otherwise I didn't want him caught because I had loved him. I didn't know which. One thing I did know: if he'd come for me now I'd have gone with him like a shot, so that doesn't say much for law and order, moral conscience and all that.

'And if they don't,' I went on, 'you'll still get the money because my mother is going to earn it and give it back.'

I waited for the derision I knew that remark would bring. It came.

'Rachel pay money back! Now you're having a joke. My guess is she's been leading you up the garden path, never did intend paying it back. "Borrow" is a word Rachel bandies around free, like herself.' Dora was vicious. I felt resentful. I believed in Mum, or thought I did. I hated it when they ran her down.

'You're like her,' Dora was saying, 'that's the trouble, you always have been. You got her blood.'

'That's not the girl's fault, Dora.' It surprised me Ron was taking my part.

My aunt, seeing she had come to a temporary end on that line, tried another.

'Where were you last night?'

'Down Mum's.'

'Why couldn't you have let me know at a proper time instead of keeping me up worrying half the night?'

'I knew you wouldn't get a message till Arthur came down in the morning, so there was nothing I could do,' I said.

'Then you should have come back home on the bus.'

That made me wonder where Tom was. I asked. Dad said he was out rabbiting with a lamp and some others. Not that he ever got anything, he wouldn't till he was allowed to borrow Ron's gun.

There seemed a lull. I thought perhaps it was over, but no.

'What none of us can forgive you, Tamsin, is stealing the money instead of asking. You know "thou shalt not steal" is one of the Lord's Commandments.'

'Yes,' I said, unbelieving. It seemed so old-fashioned somehow, like an old film. 'What would have been the good of asking?' I said. 'You wouldn't have given it.'

'We might have,' Dora lied. Then she rounded on Dad. 'Anyways, Ben, you'll have to punish her. You're her father.'

I felt my blood run cold. I'd never known what people meant when they said that before, but I knew now.

'I've said my say,' she went on,' and I'll go up. You come up too, will you, Ron. Leave Tamsin with her father.'

I jumped up, ran for the door. But my aunt was there, standing in front of it.

'You done wrong, Tamsin. You must take punishment and be grateful for it. Otherwise you'll never get to sit beside our Lord.'

She's gone crazy, I thought, I've driven her crazy. This was how she'd talked to us as children. We'd half-believed her then. I looked desperately at Ron. Wouldn't he help?

'I don't want to stay down here with Dad,' I said.

But Ron was getting his boots on. He was going out. I think he reckoned he'd said enough on my behalf. I got hold of my aunt and started to pull her away from the door.

'Take her, Ben,' she said; her voice was high, frightened.

Dad came across the room then, took me by the wrist and dragged me across to the settee. He sat down on it still keeping a hold of me. My aunt went up the stairs, closing the door behind her. At the same time Ron went out. I was alone with Dad.

He grinned at me, then he laughed.

'What you been up to, eh?' he said. 'What you been doing?' He shook his head and went on grinning and chuckling. Horrible it was. Then quite sudden, when I wasn't expecting it, he jerked me across his knee. I screamed and bit him. Perhaps it was because I bit him he hit me as hard as he did. When he let me go I could hardly stand up. I was moaning from the pain.

He was sweating from exertion. He wiped his arm

across his forehead. I swayed towards the door. I was shaking from head to foot.

'Come back,' he said. I went on. Then he was beside me.

'Kiss me, Tamsin,' he said. 'I only done it for your own good.'

His thick wet mouth came down on mine. I turned my face away and he hit me on the head. I heard a roaring, then I don't remember any more.

Ben looks down on the inert figure of Tamsin at his feet. The blurred red film in front of his eyes slowly clears, he tastes drops of salt sweat on his lips, he feels afraid. Tamsin is so still. Why doesn't she move, moan, anything to show she's alive? Fear creeps over Ben. Terror. He bends over her, touches her. She makes no response. He takes up her wrist, her pulse: nothing. She has the stillness of death about her. He must have caught her on the temple. He starts back, straightens up. He would like to shout, bellow out his agony, seize the house with his great arms and pull it down on his crime. For Ben is sure he has killed Tamsin; killed his daughter. He turns, looks round the room as though to escape from a prison, barges to the door and blunders out into the freezing mud, the darkness. The outer door stays open, the inner door swings shut as it always does, the wooden latch closing itself.

Up in her bedroom Dora kneels down on the wide, sloping floor planks and prays, or rather mumbles. She is anxious to get God on her side, to agree that she has done the right thing, the only possible thing, by insisting Ben should chastize Tamsin. Chastize is the word Dora likes to use – a bible word, one she learnt very young at Sunday-school. Didn't her father chastize her, and didn't it do her nothing but good? None of them wants Tamsin growing up like Rachel, that's for sure. Rachel has been the ruin of the family. Ben would never have taken to drink the way he has if it wasn't for Rachel. Dora is sure he wouldn't have. It is a duty not to let Tamsin follow on like her mother. She never wanted Tamsin going down there after Rachel, and now look. Exactly what she said would happen has happened. Rachel has got Tamsin in trouble. That's the way it always is with Rachel, always has been, and they – the Bands – have to suffer for it. Dora's prayers stop when she hears Tamsin scream. She scrambles to her feet and goes to the door. In the act of lifting the latch she hesitates. Ben *is* her father. If he can't do anything else he can at least punish his own daughter: that much he can do. Tamsin is too big, too strong for Dora to deal with. She needs a father. Dora lets the latch fall back into place and goes back to her kneeling position by the bed. *God*, she prays, *God help us. Give us strength.* Just now God gave her strength, strength not to go down, not to interfere, to be strong, to be cruel to be kind. If she'd been stronger with Ben he would never have married Rachel. Oh, why hadn't she been? It would have saved so much suffering for all of them. She wouldn't have had to raise Rachel's children. Here a seed of doubt creeps into a more fertile quarter of Dora's mind. Hasn't she experienced great fulfilment in raising Tom and Tamsin? Isn't Tom 'her boy'? That hour in the evening when she used come to up and say goodnight to the two little loves in the same room, read them a story from the Bible picture book: they always wanted to see the picture . . . of the Good Samaritan, and the Raising of Lazarus, and Mary and Joseph journeying to Bethlehem. Dora thinks of the difficulties she's had over the Immaculate Conception but puts them out of her mind. Mary and Joseph are different and if you don't believe that you don't believe anything – Edith agrees.

From downstairs she hears thuds and a kind of moaning. Instinctively she stiffens. What is happening? Every response in Dora inclines her to go and see, but God doesn't forsake her. He gives her strength and she remains on her knees.

She is rewarded, for she hears the front door open and close and now there is a blessed silence. Tamsin must be getting on with her homework. Ben has done what he had to do and gone out to let her think it over. Ben is sensible enough when he isn't drunk. She'll tell Ben not to let Tamsin go down there again. They've tried once, been liberal with her, and now see what. Now, unexpectedly, a serpent starts to bore its way into Dora's brain, or where Dora considers her brain to be. It asks Dora if she can be, has ever been, jealous of Rachel. No, of course she hasn't; how could any person be jealous of a no-good like Rachel? Rachel has nothing anyone could be jealous of. And in any case, she, Dora, is Ben's sister. You can't be jealous of your brother, not that kind of jealousy. That's the kind felt between man and wife. No, all she feels for Ben is the normal affection for a brother. It isn't natural not to love your brother. She wants the best for Ben, that's all. And she didn't want Rachel to take the kiddies because she knew it would do them harm. She can't be jealous of their own mother, not a poor no-good thing like Rachel. No, she's never been jealous. She can't understand people who are.

Dora's prayers are again broken in on by Tom's arrival. Dora hears him come in the front, then a long silence, then his feet come running up the stairs. She stands up quickly. She doesn't like to be caught on her knees, perhaps because the rest of the family aren't believers like she is. So when Tom bursts in, Dora is standing.

'Tamsin's fallen down,' he gasps. 'Quick!'

Panic seizes Dora. She feels she can't bear to see whatever it is she is about to. Is Tamsin dead? Had Ben taken leave of his senses and killed her? Was that why she has been praying ever since going upstairs?

'Come *on*!' Tom seizes her arm and drags her to the top of the stairs, then, seeing she is following, runs down ahead. Tamsin is lying just through the door, close to the wall. She is deathly white and neither of them are sure if she's breathing. Dora kneels down and slides her bony white hand under Tamsin's school blouse. Somewhere she must be able to feel her heart.

*

Tom's good sense takes him off without being told in search of Ron. He finds him hedging two fields over. Ron gives the slender ash a last chop which topples it, semi-severed, along the hedge, and climbs down. He walks. Tom jogs ahead, imploring him to hurry. Ron never runs but he is walking very fast, as fast as Tom's jog. He doesn't ask questions, he's got the message. What was Ben thinking of? What's he done to the girl? And where was Dora? Dora must have been there in the house. Ron had been in two minds whether to interfere, tell Dora to let the girl be, tell Ben to leave her, but it wasn't his business when you came to look at it. Ben is her father and Dora has raised her. The farm is his business, not the children. Though he likes them, mind. The place won't be the same when they're grown and gone. That's the trouble. Dora and Ben can't accept Tamsin is grown – pretty nearly. She isn't a kid you can spank any longer. So what the hell has Ben been doing knocking her about? For that is what Ron feels sure has happened.

They reach the house. Inside, Dora is kneeling, weeping and praying beside Tamsin, who lies as before. In moments of crisis like this Dora doesn't mind being found on her knees. Indeed, if the others as well would get down and kneel with her, God would probably make Tamsin better.

Ron does kneel, but to feel Tamsin's pulse, which beats strongly if somewhat irregularly. He sends Dora upstairs for blankets and a hot bottle. Tom puts the kettle over, then runs with coins from the kitchen drawer to the telephone-box at the top of the lane. Dr Ash, he is told, is out on his rounds but they will try to get a message to him. Tom is peeing himself with agitation and fear. He looks down at his wet leg and the pool at his feet. It's urgent, he says. The voice asks if he wants the hospital. Tom is afraid of hospitals and doesn't know whether he wants it. Hurry up, says the voice, there are expectant mothers in the clinic waiting for their ante-natal exercises. Yes, says Tom, he does want the hospital. Then I'll cancel the call for Dr Ash, says the voice. No, says Tom, desperate, he wants both.

The voice tells him icily that Dr Ash won't come if he knows it is in the hands of the hospital, where Dr Perry is in charge. Tom plumps for Dr Perry and the hospital after seconds of indecision, then wishes he hasn't – Dr Ash is their doctor. Dr Ash won't go for them about cleaning up the house and putting slates on the roof. The hospital answers: is it an emergency? Can Tom get her to the outpatients department, casualty ward? No, his dad's not around and he's the only one who can drive. Very well then, if he's sure it's an emergency they'll send an ambulance. Tom loses courage; he isn't sure. He puts down the receiver, dials again for the clinic. Could they get the message to Dr Ash? He gives Tamsin's name yet again and the name of the farm. Very well, they will do what they can, but if the hospital doesn't think it necessary to send out an ambulance then—

'Please,' Tom gasps, 'please send Dr Ash as quick as he can come.'

He puts down the receiver, gives a last glance at the pool on the floor, wedges the door open with a stone so people will think it's rain blown in, and runs back down the lane.

When he gets there Tamsin is wrapped up and laid on the chaise-longue pulled out from its cobwebby corner. As he comes in she looks at him. Tom sighs with relief that the ambulance isn't coming.

Rachel is holding her pay miraculously given her by her boss. She half-expected it would be cut off, but now the coppers have quite decided it is Joe, Rachel's name is cleared – more or less. At the same time her boss has given her notice, told her to go by the end of the month. That's two weeks. He's closing the garage down, he says.

As Rachel stands in her not-very-clean room (she has given up cleaning it since Joe left) she contemplates whether or not to return Tamsin the £50. She has only £60. With this £60 she can go to London, start a new life, find Joe perhaps. This last is the main incentive, in spite of the long odds. Rachel is nothing if not optimistic. She hopes that Joe's friend who has got work in Cornwall will eventually hear from Joe, and that she will track him that way. She looks down at the notes again, held together by an elastic band. She flicks them through. All except one are Tamsin's by right; or rather, the farm's. But doesn't the farm owe her something? Shouldn't Ben have given her something when she first left him, at least? She has never had one single penny out of the place whereas they've lived off it all these years; lived well too, judging by the way Tamsin's dressed.

A momentary regret comes to her: Tom. She would like to have seen Tom. Not got intimate with him like she has with Tamsin, but just seen him, what he looked like, out of curiosity.

Oddly enough this last consideration is quite a deterrent to Rachel. It almost changes her mind. It leads her on to thinking about Tamsin; and her heart, if not her mind, swings the other way on the pendulum. She knows from the police's questions that Joe and Tamsin spent the night before he ran off together somewhere up on the moor. Little bitch, she thinks, rotten little bitch. Knowing how much Joe meant to her it was a mean trick. Even if Tamsin did love him, Rachel thinks, it can't be the same way that *she* has because at that age you just don't love the same way as when you're older. When you're in your teens its mainly flattery and curiosity . . . and stupidity (thinking of herself and Ben). Now Rachel considers the quality of her love altogether different. It doesn't occur to her that loving Joe is even stupider than loving Ben although her love may be more obsessive, wholehearted and desperate. What her instinct does tell her is that she has had something special with Joe she'll never find again, and that's true enough. Something special is never repeated. You can't just walk round the corner and find it again with someone else, sadly. That's what the young think, but not Rachel. Rachel has lived long enough to know.

So she puts the notes in her purse and snaps it shut. Tamsin has deprived her of her last night with Joe, probably her last night ever; Tamsin can pay – literally, in every sense. Again Rachel hesitates. This means she won't see Tamsin again, won't even say goodbye, which seems a bit tough on the kid. But there, that's life. Rachel walks round picking up ashtrays and emptying them in a paper bag. She won't think any more, it doesn't do any good. She'll pack her bag, take a bus into Exeter first thing tomorrow morning, and a coach on up to London. Once she's earning again, she'll send Tamsin the money. At this thought the frown of anxiety disappears from Rachel's forehead. There is nothing now to impede her resolution. She goes out to the garage and fetches a broom.

Dr Ash turns his black 1950 Daimler down the narrow lane to Ventnor. He accepts philosophically the thorn and bramble that stretch out from the banks to claw his shiny roof and doors. He's used to such lanes, goes up and down them twice a week on his rounds, but this is one of the worst. The last time he remembers coming out to the Bands' was after the boy was born to Ben Band's wife. He has often thought about that young woman living down in Ventnor. She didn't strike him as the right sort for a life like the Bands lead – a life not untypical of a good many tucked away in the moor valleys, it is true, but the Bands are almost a clan. They keep to themselves for the most part. You seldom see them out except for Miss Band down at the market. He has heard Ben Band is on to the hard stuff.

His concentration comes back to the lane. The bridge is so narrow he must swing into it at exactly the right angle or he will scrape the sides of his car on the low granite parapet. And granite's not like brambles. The long, rather sinister-looking car eases its way over the bridge, up the small incline and into Ventnor yard. Dr Ash winds down his window, wound up to protect him from the brambles, and looks with depression at the territory he must traverse if he is to reach the door. This is the very reason his younger colleague will not go out to see his patients but insists they come to him or are fetched by ambulance. Dr Ash doesn't agree – he has seen too much. Besides he learns far more about his patients and why they are ill if he sees them in their home setting. It stands to reason. How is he to tell them one from another, understand what they tell him about themselves, or where the pain comes from, unless he sees how they live? Lined up in the clinic they all look like peas in a pod. Oh yes, he can hand them out pills and prescriptions but he can't really know what's wrong with them.

He opens the door, lifts a pair of wellingtons from the passenger side and, seated sideways, undoes his shoes and pulls on the boots. That done he stands up in the squelching black mud and wades carefully towards the house, carrying his shoes. Dr Ash knows better than to be hurried. He's had an accident in such conditions before now.

He reaches the door at the same moment as it opens. They have heard the car, and if they hadn't heard it they would certainly have felt it. There's a sort of second sight in families like the Bands; the doctor has come to accept this fact after years of practising amongst them. He nods to Miss Band, sits on the bench built into the porch on either side, removes his boots and puts on his shoes. He straightens up slowly. His back is not what it was but he supposes it inevitable at sixty-three. Still, he's glad to say, his other faculties seem as good as ever. He now looks at Miss Band's face, which reveals little – relief, perhaps, that he has come. Head bent to miss the low doorway, he enters the dark interior. A girl is lying on the old chaise: Tamsin Band, no doubt. She doesn't move but lies flat on her back looking up at him with big anxious eyes out of a white face.

Dr Ash never wastes words except when he feels like talking, preferably about cricket. Right now he looks round for a hook to hang his coat. Miss Band obliges and takes it from him. Mr Band is by the stove. He's not the brother that drinks, Dr Ash can tell that at a glance. A boy hovers by the table – possibly the boy of the mother he saw some years back. It doesn't seem long.

He crosses to the chaise and sits down on the edge.

Tamsin shifts a little to make room for him.

'So you're the patient.' He smiles down kindly on Tamsin. He has a propensity for the young and the old.

Tamsin likes him, she trusts him. She lies quietly enough while he takes her pulse.

'That's all right.' He looks round at the others. 'If the rest of you would care to leave us, I'd like to talk to Tamsin and give her a checking over. Stay if you like, Miss Band.'

Ron and Tom troop out. Dora hesitates.

'You can make me a cup of tea,' says the doctor to put her at ease. She's very strung up, he observes. He turns back to Tamsin.

Tamsin too appears anxious and wary, despite her attempt to smile.

'Now,' he says, 'tell me what's the trouble.'

Dora chips in.

'She fell down the stair and hit her head. She was stretched out there when I come down.'

'So you hit your head when you fell? How did an active young lass like you come to fall down the stairs, eh?'

Dr Ash reaches out his expert fingers and feels Tamsin's head. She winces. He parts her hair, looks more closely at her scalp.

'It's certainly taken a knock,' he comments.

'She was unconscious,' Dora adds. 'When Tom found her, he thought she was dead.'

'So Tom found her?'

'Tom found her and came up to tell me.'

Dr Ash is silent for a few moments, his stethoscope on Tamin's chest.

'You didn't hear any sound of Tamsin falling down the stairs? You don't know how long she'd been lying there when Tom found her?'

Dora flushes.

'I had my door shut, doctor.'

He tells Tamsin to sit up and turn her back. He wants to listen to her breathing. Tamsin hesitates, unfastens her blouse and then turns her back. She is still wearing her skirt, but unbuttoned, and as she bends forward a red welt reveals itself. Then another. The doctor says nothing; he listens to her breathing. That done he asks Dora to leave them a few moments. Dora hesitates. The doctor looks at her expectantly. She goes up the stairs.

Dr Ash turns back to Tamsin, his hands on his knees. He looks at her. She returns his look then drops heavy lids over her eyes.

'What's been going on out here, eh?'

No reply.

'Do you mean to tell me those marks across your back were caused by falling down the stairs?'

Tamsin's white face flushes scarlet. She says nothing.

'Where's your dad?'

'Out.'

'When did he go out?'

Tamsin doesn't know. She hasn't seen him since she got back this evening. The doctor is pretty sure she's lying, but thinks it unlikely to have been the other Band brother. It certainly couldn't have been the aunt, she wouldn't have had the strength.

'I ought to take you in the hospital – let them make a proper report on you.'

Terror is written all over Tamsin's face.

'Do you want me to?'

'No.' Tamsin is quite clear.

The doctor picks up his bag, then hesitates.

'Does this kind of thing happen often?'

Tamsin stares at him, then shakes her head, wincing as she does so.

The doctor makes one last attempt. He leans forward over the chaise.

'Tell me what happened.'

'I fell down the stairs,' Tamsin answers.

He claps his hands on his knees, stands up. 'So be it,' he says. He opens the stair door. Miss Band is standing at the top. She comes down.

'Keep her where she is for three days,' he says. 'Keep her

warm and quiet. I'll leave an ointment to put on those bruises. If she gets any headache, ring the hospital immediately to send out for her.'

He pulls open the door into the porch and sits down to take off his shoes.

'Shut the door, Miss Band,' he says. 'I'd like a word with you.'

Dora moves into the porch, shutting the door behind her.

'It doesn't look to me like a fall down the stairs your niece is suffering from.'

Dora's hands move nervously.

'If you care to make a claim against either of your brothers, the marks on her body will be evidence enough.'

Dora continues to move her hands and twitch.

'It was a fall, doctor. No more. An accident, like. No one pushed her, I'd swear to that.'

Dr Ash stands up, complete with bag and boots, shoes in hand. He can see he's making no progress. He knows it's no use him saying any more. If he does, next time the same sort of thing occurs they won't even call him. He's probably said too much already, but he's no grounds for taking further action, unless Tamsin or the aunt make some kind of claim.

He starts his wade back through the mud to his car. He fervently wishes it would stop raining – at least the mud freezes over in the cold.

Two days I lay quiet in my bed; the third my aunt went down to Taverston and I was up soon as she was gone. I'd been doing school work for my 'O's to pass the time, but what was on my mind was Mum. I wanted to go to London with her. The more I thought about it, the more I was sure I had to go. It seemed the only way I could get away from Dad. The one thing I was certain of was I couldn't go on living under the same roof as him. So soon as I was up, I went off up the hill to the phone-box and rang Mum.

She must have been out at the pumps because she took a

long time coming. When she did answer she sounded hurried, a bit impatient.

'Mum,' I said, 'I have to come up to London with you.'

There was a long pause.

'How's that?' she said at last.

'I can't stick it with Dad,' I said. 'I can't go living with him no longer.'

'I don't know exactly when I'm going,' she said. I knew she didn't want me. I bit my lip to keep my voice steady.

'Mum,' I said, 'don't you care about me a bit?'

'Course I do,' she said, quick. 'But I don't think we'll have the money.'

'Not with that I gave you?' I said. 'We could go on borrowing it longer.' I was desperate. I didn't care any more about paying it back nor nothing. 'Please, Mum,' I said. 'Dad's been hitting me about.'

'What for?' she said.

'For taking the money,' I said.

The pips went in the silence and I pushed in another five.

'OK,' she says. 'Come along Friday and we'll catch the early train Saturday.'

'Thanks,' I said. 'Thanks, Mum.' And that was it.

I left the phone-box and set off walking. I felt happy as could be, happier than I'd ever felt before – except maybe with Joe and that was a different kind. It didn't seem to matter what I did, so I wandered back down the lane, pulling grasses out the hedge and chewing them. There was no wind to speak of, the sky was a clear hard blue with a jet trail stretching across it like a lamb's-tail. There were real lambs in the fields too. Lambing had started in a big way. Ron was bringing them in all the time. When I reached the yard, I looked over the stable door at two doubles kept in with their mothers. I wondered whether or not I should put them out but reckoned I'd better not without asking Ron; instead I thought I'd follow down the stream, then up past Higher Wellshead to the miners' pool set back into the moor among the old disused shaft-heads. The thought did cross my mind it was a bit far and I shouldn't be doing too much, but I wanted to go so there it was.

I dillydallied by the stream a good while. The undergrowth was flattened by snow and rain. It was always flattened at this time of year. I could follow right along the bank, swinging round the tree-trunks and keeping out of the muddy tracks the cattle had made. Birds were singing and flittering about from bush to bush, tiny wrens ticking at me for coming on their ground, and robins hopping about and watching. Wagtails too were on the rocks in the stream, bobbing and seeming as though they were coming along with me.

After about a half-hour I left the stream and climbed up on to the moor. It was a fair climb and I was quite out of breath by the time I came over the top of the ridge and saw the pool. It was blue as the sky in the centre with masses of dark, yellowy-red weed round the edges, and still as a glass. It took your breath away set in there between the brown-black hills that went sweeping away on either side. Ahead, the stream wriggled on up between turf and heather till the valley sloped up into a kind of punch-bowl and that was the head of it. A few hill sheep were about like they always are on the moor, but otherwise there was nothing moving in sight, neither cattle, nor ponies, nor humans. I had the place to myself – except for the birds. Three buzzards were wheeling up above the valley, crying their strange, lonely call. Little birds were hopping round the pond, lots I didn't know the names of. I lay down on a rock on my stomach so I could look down in the water and look out round. I really felt happy, like singing, only I can't sing. Up above larks were doing it for me. I rolled over on my back to try to see them, but I didn't stay that way long – it was too painful. It set me to thinking about Dad again, it was like a black cloud coming in front of the sun.

He hadn't come home since he walked out the house. I was relieved. Each day I dreaded him coming. For my aunt it was different; she listened to every sound in the yard expecting it to be him. I knew she couldn't be at peace for worrying about him, although it wasn't the first time he'd been gone two days. I couldn't see the need to get fussed up for nothing. Ron wasn't, I was sure of that.

Two ravens passed over me flying high, croaking, one came down on top of the other; the lower one dropped, rolled over on its back and slipped away. I looked down in the pool and saw their shadows leaving it and going up over the turf the far side. A sheep bleated just behind me, like an old grandmother coughing; it made me start. I lay there for a long time, dreaming Joe was there with me, wondering if I'd see him in London, wondering how much my mother knew. I went back over the night in the car together and the feel came back over me as real as if he was there . . . I think I must have almost gone to sleep for the next thing I knew I was cold and stiff. I stood up quickly. The sun was much lower and the hills behind me were in shadow. The place didn't seem quite so friendly now: the pool had turned dark. It felt a bit lonely and I shivered. I was just about to step off the rock and go back down when I saw something that made me freeze with terror and horror. My heart gave a thump and seemed to stop. It was a hand and arm, not far from me, but not the way I'd been facing, sticking up out of the edge of the weeds. I stood there for I don't know how long staring at it. I couldn't move. I knew the person must be drowned but I didn't know for how long; for all I knew someone could have come up and drowned themselves while I slept on the rock. Supposing they're not drowned, I thought, supposing if I pulled them out now I could save them?

It was the last thing in the world I wanted to do, but I had to. I went down as near as I could get on the bank, then I rolled my jeans up above my knees and put a foot in. The cold of the water was painful, agony, but I had to reach that hand quick. I took a step forward and went down up to the top of my thighs. I was scared. I can't swim. I reached forward. I could just touch the stiff fingers. I gave a little pull. It came easy, the body, through the water towards me.

It was Dad. I think I'd known all along.

I stumbled back to the bank towing him behind me. His face was horrible and bloated. I didn't even try to get him out. When I saw he must have been drowned a day or more, I let him go. I turned round and was sick in the bracken; for a bit I could think of nothing for the sickness. Then I stood up unsteadily and ran. I never looked at him again. It wasn't so much his face I remembered, it was that sticking-up hand. All the way home I thought what he must have been through, the terrible icy pain of the water, then his lungs filling and that hand clutching, clutching at what? Weeds?

Dad couldn't swim no more'n I can.

I didn't stop till I was just outside the farm, then for the first time I wondered what I was going to say. How was I to tell my aunt? She'd go nuts. Then I saw there was no lights on so I guessed she wasn't back. I went in, up to my room and got out of my wet clothes. My teeth were chattering with cold. I ran the bath. Because my aunt had been out all day, the water was hot. It took me ages getting into it.

Tom, walking down the lane from the school bus, stops to look over the valley through a gap in the hedge. Not that Tom's one to look at views; he can't see anything to them, but he likes to see out over, see where everyone is. From where he is now he can see the farm and the yard settled into the hill opposite, the trees twisting along beside the stream, the acres of bog-grass stretching down the wide open valley, some of them dotted with the dark green of spruce seedlings. A flash of silver shows him where the school bus has reached in the lane. He looks away from that. He's had enough of school, he's no scholar.

Back across the valley the farm is in shadow. No smoke is coming from the chimney. But up behind, the fields are in sun still and the sky is white where it meets the black ridge of the moor. It gets bluer and bluer as it gets higher. Tom looks at the sun and blinks. He rubs his eyes, looks lower this time and sees Ron in the corner of a field with a ewe:

lambing. Tom wonders idly how many lambs there are now, then his attention is caught by someone moving along between the hedges. He can't quite see who it is but he sees them through the gaps in the bank when their head shows up through. It looks like Tamsin but she's supposed to be sick as far as Tom knows, in bed. He climbs the bars of the gate in front of him to see better.

It *is* Tamsin and she's running. Tom doesn't wait to see more; he slings his satchel over his shoulder and walks on down the lane. He wonders, without really knowing he's doing so, if his father's back. Not that he cares one way or the other. he just wonders.

When he nears the house, the chill of the shadow makes him hurry the last stretch to the door and go straight in. Inside's a disappointment, it's not much warmer than out. Tom opens the stove door, looks in, sees a few red embers in the bottom, opens the draught, riddles it and puts in some sticks. Then he hears a tap running in the bath up above. He listens, amazed. No one ever has a bath at Ventnor except at night, and then not often. It must be Tamsin. He opens the stair door and shouts up.

'Tamsin?'

The water sloshes around. He hears sounds of her getting out.

'What you doing?'

'What d'you think?'

'Where's everyone?'

Silence.

Tom gives up. He never can understand his sister. It's the kind of nutty thing she *would* do, have a bath in the middle of the day when their aunt is out. Otherwise there'd be trouble, wasting hot water for no reason. He saunters out of the dark house and climbs the hill to look for Ron up with the sheep in the sun.

'I don't know, I'm sure, how you stand it like you do.'

Edith is sitting, cup poised, in front of a teapot decorated by roses and cornflowers. She brushes a crumb of home-made cake off the white crocheted cloth made by herself, and restores the tea-cosy, made by her daughter, to the pot.

Dora, opposite, puts her own empty cup down in front of her. She has come round to Edith's in the hope of hearing news of Ben, but Edith has heard nothing. Dora is nervous, agitated. She is anxious to be off. Perhaps by now Ben will be home, but it isn't easy to get away from Edith. She has already had to eat two slices of cake she didn't want and listen to a detailed account of Edith's niece's unfortunate experience in the maternity unit. Dora is getting desperate.

She tries to stand but her button is caught in the crocheted cloth. An appalling accident to Edith's tea-set is only just avoided, after which Edith insists she have another cup of tea. Dora gives way.

'Seems to me that one'll be back soon enough, same as he always is. I can't see why you worry yourself silly like you do.' Edith pours a steady stream into the cornflower cup.

Dora sits stiffly. She cannot, could never, describe the state of Tamsin's back and lower, and if she did . . . She shudders at the very thought. No, never. It is a dark secret that must stay in the family along with other skeletons shut in the cupboard under the stair. There are some things that can never be told, must go with her to the grave, Dora has decided long since. Ben's over-punishment – for that's how Dora sees it – of Tamsin is one of them.

'I must get back to Tamsin, anyways,' she says, standing again, this time with greater care. 'She's not right yet.'

'Sounded nasty from what I heard,' Edith says. Dora freezes. What has Edith heard?

'She fell from top to bottom,' Dora says. 'You know what our stairs are like.'

'Bruised all up her back, I heard.'

'Who did you hear from?' Dora quivers.

'Mr Tomey told me in the chemists.'

Dora knows that Edith has guessed, but no admission shall ever cross Dora's lips. Edith, to Edith's dissatisfaction, will never do more than suspect.

Dora says goodbye and leaves. Her bicycle is left against the bank at the top of the rough lane to the road. She mounts it and pedals up the gently mounting road in the fading light. One small star twinkles ahead of her. Perhaps it is guiding her to Ben. Perhaps when she goes in Ventnor kitchen Ben will be sitting there beside the stove waiting for her. Dora's heart leaps with joy and anticipation. She loves Ben, she loves Ben – another secret that must go with her to the grave, though it is natural enough isn't it, him being one of the family? Dora pedals harder.

I lay in the bath with my teeth chattering until bit by bit the heat seeped into me. Even so my teeth kept on for quite a while longer. I hadn't known how cold I was till I met the hot water. I stayed in a long while till it got cold and I heard Tom come in. I dreaded getting out. I dreaded meeting anyone. What was I going to say? 'Dad's drowned up in the miners' pool.' Was that what I'd say? Flat, just like that? I couldn't bear the thought of saying it. I couldn't bear the thought of their faces; my aunt's most of all. I hated watching other people shocked and suffering; I knew that was how my aunt would look. I felt sick at the thought. I didn't want to be the one to tell her. Perhaps I could tell Ron, and Ron would tell her. When I thought some more I didn't want to tell Ron either, nor Tom, nor anyone. Why couldn't I keep quiet and let someone else find him? Wouldn't that be the best way? That way it wouldn't be so much of a shock. They'd get used to him being gone; it would come gradual like. The more I thought about it, the better the idea seemed. Someone was bound to come across Dad pretty soon, dragged up to the bank the way I'd left him. There were people up there riding often enough, and farmers looking at their sheep. So I wouldn't say a thing, I'd just wait till someone else brought the news. Dad was dead, wasn't he? Nothing I said now would make any difference, one way or the other – it was just they'd hear a bit later. And later seemed to me a lot better. After all, if I hadn't chanced to walk up to the pool I'd never found him and no one'd ever have been the wiser.

I saw my wet clothes lying on the bathroom floor spreading a puddle. I had to do something about them. I put them in the bath, rinsed them out and wrung them. Then I was stuck: if I put them in any of the normal places to dry my aunt'd see them. Oh well, I'd just say I'd washed them. I went to my room and got on some dry clothes, then I went back and heaped the wet ones in a bucket and took them though to my room. I put them behind the wardrobe; I'd hang them out the day after. Then I went downstairs and leaned over the stove for warmth. I was feeling cold again. Tom was at the table sticking together some bits of whittled wood.

'What you having a bath for?' he said soon as he saw me.

'I felt like it,' I said. 'Why not?'

'Thought you were supposed to be ill,' he said.

'So what?' I said.

'Saw you running pretty quick along the lane just now.'

My heart missed a beat. So I'd been seen – even if it was only Tom. I hadn't been going to say I'd been out at all.

'I wasn't running,' I said.

'Looked like you was.'

Tom is obstinate. He's the most obstinate person I know.

'Well I wasn't,' I said.

He didn't answer for a bit. He seemed absorbed in what he was making. Then he said:

'We'll ask Ron if you wasn't running when he comes in.' I panicked.

'How do you know Ron saw me?' I asked sharp.

'Must have,' said Tom, placid like. 'He was in the field just up above. Reefers.' All our fields have names, and it's true if he'd been in Reefers he must have seen me.

'I didn't see him,' I said.

156

'You wasn't looking, was you?' Tom commented, running a tube of glue along one stick and pushing it down tight on another.

'Anyways,' he said, looking up now, 'what does it matter if he saw you running along the lane?'

'It doesn't,' I said, casual. 'It's just that I promised Auntie I wouldn't go out. She'll be mad at me. So don't say . . . unless Ron does.'

'OK,' said Tom. He's all right really once he can see reason, but you can't be sure when he isn't going to forget.

'Don't forget,' I said, threatening, 'or I'll think of something you don't want me to tell.'

I seemed childish listening to myself, but then I was talking to a child. That's how I explained it to myself. Actually I was dead scared. I knew I ought to tell about Dad, it was obvious to tell. Perhaps I would. Yet I couldn't hear myself doing it.

Then Auntie came in. I heard her getting off her boots in the porch, leaving them there. If I'm going to say I'll have to say now, I thought. But I couldn't, not straight out like that. I couldn't. I'll let her get settled, sit down, I thought. She took off her coat and looked at me.

'Aren't you lying down?' she asked.

'I have been,' I said, 'but I got sick of it.'

She looked at the other pegs where Ron and Ben kept their coats and caps.

'Your dad not back?' she asked, though she could see by the empty peg and the empty chair by the stove.

'No,' I said. I opened my mouth then to tell her. I was going to. I was really, when she said:

'He's been seen about. I heard from Edith, who heard from her cousin.'

So I didn't say anything. I know I was crazy but I couldn't. Why is it there are some things you can't say? You just *can't say them.*

My aunt was going on.

'If you're up you might as well go out the garden, fetch

me a cabbage. Ron'll want something cooked and Ben may be back, so I'll cook up something hot.'

I felt dizzy. The kitchen was going round me and up and down like a roundabout. I went out to fetch the cabbage. I felt better out there where the air was cold and clear and a star twinkled low in the dip of the valley. I'll say later, I thought; later, when Ron's in too.

It was while I was cutting the cabbage I got the idea: I wouldn't go back in the house, I'd go to my mother right away. I'd never tell them what I'd seen that day.

The walk over the moor was all right to start with, while the sky was still light and there was a half-moon up, but the moon set early and clouds came up over the stars. I made my way by the feel of my feet on the hard surface under them, and by the lighter sky showing through the dark trees on the banks. But after a little the sky became as black as all the rest. I'd hoped I'd get a lift, but the two cars I did thumb drove straight past; maybe they didn't see me till late, maybe they didn't fancy picking someone up at night. I kept walking. Up on the top there was more wind and it was then I began to get panicky – not of anything exactly, but of . . . ghosts, spirits, I don't know what. I thought I heard footsteps behind me and I went quicker; the steps seemed to come quicker too. I stopped. They stopped. I think it was the blood pumping through my ears, but I couldn't get it out of my head it was Dad. Then something shadowy stepped out in the road ahead of me and I thought I should die for fear. It was a pony.

Another time I heard breathing right by me and ran for nearly a mile, again sure it was Dad. Perhaps he wasn't drowned after all, perhaps he'd recovered and was coming after me. But in my heart I knew he was dead. It was his ghost I was afraid of. If I was ever haunted it was by Dad that night.

When I got to where the inn is supposed to have slipped down a mine-shaft overnight and left a ghost patrolling the stretch of road beside it, I could hardly face to go on. I knew I was going to see it and it would look like Dad. I'd have to go round, or back. But back was nearly as far as on, and round over the rocks and rough ground was nearly impossible at night without a torch. I didn't know the territory like I did round home.

Halfway along that stretch I heard a car. I put out my arm and stood out a bit in the headlights. It stopped. I ran up. He was going to Asherford. I sank back in the seat, I was so relieved I could hardly speak, but I answered the questions he asked. He was a farmer coming back from a meeting he'd been to the other side of the moor. He set me down by the bridge outside the garage. It wasn't that late. I saw on his car clock twenty to ten near as not. I thanked him and he drove off.

The door was locked. I walked round the back: no light, nothing. Everything was dark and black. Blackness seemed to be closing round. I tapped on the window. Perhaps Mum had gone to bed early, perhaps I only had to wake her and the lights would come on, everything would be all right. But I tapped in vain. I looked round me. There was a light on in an upstairs window across the bridge and a lamplight further along the street. Otherwise everything was silent in that strange shut way of villages at night. Not that it being awake would have made much difference to me, but its shutness made me feel lonelier, more isolated. I didn't know what to do. I couldn't get back to the farm, that was certain, and I didn't like to barge in on Denise's family at night without an invitation; besides it was a further two miles' walk.

I wandered round the back of the workshop and out in the yard. Here there was no light at all, not even a street lamp, so I had to feel my way between the old scrap cars till I got my fingers on a door that opened easily. It was beginning to rain. I crawled in the front, then over to the back seat. It had that peculiar smell of old cars, damp and must mixed up with the smell of old upholstery. I stretched out along the seat. There was no doubt in my mind this was where I'd have to spend the night. Soon, from way off down the street, I heard shouts and singing. Closing time I thought, only half-past ten and I had the whole night stretching ahead of me. I wondered if I'd ever sleep. I'd have to go back to the farm the next day, I knew that. My mother had betrayed me, that's how I saw it. She'd gone to London I was sure, without even telling me or saying goodbye. I wondered if she'd write. It didn't seem like I slept at all that long cold night, but I suppose there must have been times when I dozed. Then at last I looked up and could see the shape of the window frame against the grey outside, and the shape of a wooded hill beyond. I was never so pleased to see the dawn.

Ben has been gone now for five days. Every night Dora goes for Ron, tells him he should report it to the police. Ron doesn't, nor does Dora. They never have been people for telling the police.

Tamsin's back in school. She went straight there on the bus from Asherford after her night spent in the car. She's moody and silent, but there. Her teacher breathes a sigh of relief, perhaps it is not yet too late to reclaim Tamsin Band for her 'O's. But after a day or two she becomes despondent. Tamsin is not concentrating. She remembers nothing she is told – and a good memory, after all, is how exams are passed.

Tom is the only one actively occupied in finding his father. He sits upstairs in the evening after school dangling his needle on a thread over his map. Several times it has seemed to stop and circle over the moor, somewhere up over Barrowdown. Tom goes out up the lane where he saw Tamsin running back that day. He gets as far as the gate where the lane crosses a field and then continues up to the moor, but somehow he can't bring himself to go further. He isn't stupid, he's connected up Tamsin's wet clothes found by her aunt behind the wardrobe and Tamsin's running off down her mother's last Thursday with something that's happened up on the moor. So he hangs over the gate, looking at the ridge, and a nasty feeling comes over him – a feeling of disgust, of dread, of something Tamsin knows about and he can't face to go and look for. For Tom is a bit psychic, he feels already how he'll feel when he finds . . . 'it', whatever it is. Hanging over the gate on this grey day Tom is beginning to know his father is dead. He won't admit it to himself or put it in words, but he's stopped working at school, he's getting in trouble. Every evening he comes home and dashes straight up to his bedroom for his pendulum, hoping, always hoping, it'll show something different. But no, it always circles over exactly the same place.

Ron goes on the same as usual. There's the farm to think of. The animals still have to be seen to, whatever else happens. But when evening comes he can't rest in his mind. Ben was a burden when there, but he's more of a burden now he's gone. It wouldn't be so bad if it wasn't for Dora pacing up and down like a sleepwalker. She goes to chapel every day to pray for Ben's return. She goes to Edith a lot too. She has to talk to someone after all. None of them at home are any good for talking, not *real* talking, about what's on your mind. Edith tries her best to help, but news of Ben is scarce. At first people kept remembering where they'd seen him, but now . . .

'You should go to the police,' Edith says to Dora. And Dora agrees; but doesn't go. For she too, like Tom, is sure that something terrible has happened to Ben, so what good would the police be if Ben is—? No, she can't say it; she shuts the possibility out of her mind but she stops nagging Ron to search. In fact now she talks very little, except to Edith and Tamsin about the wickedness of Rachel and the missing £50.

Then, on the sixth day, when March has gone and April is just beginning in a cold fashion with daffodils bending and nodding in the violent gusts of wind, Constable Jenkins drives down the lane one evening with another copper sitting beside him. Tamsin's not home from school. Tom sees them from his bedroom window. At first he freezes with apprehension, but curiosity soon thaws his legs and takes him down to the kitchen. He hasn't, after all, loved his dad; no child really could. It may not even be about his dad the coppers have come, but Tom is sure it is. Two of them in a car instead of the copper alone on his bike – that's never happened before in Tom's lifetime.

When Tom enters the kitchen, Constable Jenkins is standing awkwardly holding his hat, and his aunt is sitting white as a sheet. Ron also has his cap off; he stares fixedly, more owl-like than usual, through his round glasses. Tom looks from one to another. He supposes the other copper has stayed with the car.

His aunt beckons him to her, puts her arm round him and draws him close – a thing Tom hates, but he doesn't like to pull away.

'Your dad's dead, Tom—' She suddenly buries her face in Tom's chest and weeps. Tom stands stiff, dry-eyed and acutely embarrassed. The constable looks embarrassed too. Ron polishes his glasses, breathes on them.

'If you'd care to come along now, Mr Band, for the identification.'

Dora pulls her face out of Tom's chest to tell Ron his suit's in the landing cupboard. Ron goes up to change.

Meanwhile the constable sees fit to give some details to Tom, Miss Band's grief preventing her.

'Found him up at the miners' pool, up the top there about four mile along the down. Wally White seen the body in the edge of the water when he was up after his sheep. Made his stomach turn he said. He guessed who't was. Came straight and rang in the station and we come out. We walked in from the other road.'

Constable Jenkins would like to go on in further detail: the problems of moving a decomposed body from a pond a car couldn't get anywhere near; the need for a caterpillar tractor etcetera; it is not often in his area he has a murder or suicide to liven things up. But his finer feelings make him refrain from saying more in front of Tom. Tom remains mute. He stands stolidly by his aunt with his eyes fixed on

162

an area of peeling paint above the mantel. Only that way can Tom keep some kind of hold on his toppling world. His dad is gone, and however bad he was, however much dreaded, it is a loss to Tom's stability, his set-up. His home is radically altered, can never be the same again. Shock imprints itself for life on Tom's impressionable person, although Tom doesn't know it.

Ron comes down the stairs dressed in his best and he and the constable go out to the waiting car. Dora and Tom hear it reverse, turn, and pull away.

I knew they'd found Dad by Ron coming and fetching me home from school in the car. He almost never drove. I guessed at once the reason. It was not until we'd gone round the roundabout and were going along the stretch of flat past the horse-racing stables that he said:

'They've found your dad.'

'Where?' I asked, automatic.

'Drowned up at the miners' pool,' he said. 'Wally White come on him.'

I thought we were going home but when we got to the Y-fork he took the right turn for Meridan.

'Where are we going?' I asked.

'Police station.'

'What for?' Fear made my stomach turn over. I felt sweat start to come up on me.

'Questioning,' he said, brief. 'You don't need to fuss. Don't tell 'em nothing save what they know already. See?'

'Yes,' I said. I wondered what Ron thought I knew. 'What about Tom?' I asked.

When we got to the police station Ron came up the steps with me, but at the door a copper took me in and Ron went back to the car. I was taken in the chief's office. The social worker was there sat in the corner, I knew her from before. Nosy all of us thought she was, but then I suppose it was her business to be. The sight of her dried me up good and proper, even more than the chief. He was kind in spite of asking me the same questions over and over in different ways. Our local copper was standing there listening to everything and twitching. He was the one who'd gone up the pool about Dad.

The long and short of it was I didn't tell them anything, anything but what I cared to tell. I wasn't going to admit to finding Dad up at the pool because that was locked away inside me for good, along with the other things about Dad and me nobody knew. It was them getting wind I was lying that made them keep on and on with the questioning. They didn't keep me long that evening, but they came out the farm the next day and asked me the same questions and a whole lot more. My aunt was there because they weren't allowed to question me on my own.

They questioned her after, and Ron and Tom. I was desperate to know what they'd said but I didn't dare ask for fear they'd realize I knew more than I'd told them and they'd let on to the police. I felt pretty sure I was safe with Ron. I wasn't so sure about Tom. I mean how can you know what a kid of eleven'll say? And when it came to my aunt I was dead scared. I knew she'd suffered over Dad, and the good Lord would always be at her shoulder nudging her to come out with what she'd call truth. So in the end I settled for sticking to my story. I reckoned there was no way they could ever know I'd been up to the pool and found Dad because I was certain, as certain as you ever can be on the moor, that I hadn't been seen. The only thing that worried me was if I'd been seen coming back along the lane. So I said I'd been out and wandered along to see if there was any new lambs, just in case.

Two weeks later they held the inquest.

7 April 1975

The coroner has a house on the outskirts of Taverston. He is anxious to get the inquest on the death of Benjamin Band over as quickly as possible so that he may return to the problem of mowing a lawn decorated by moorland boulders. The moor is his wife's hobby. With a jury of seven, he has opened the inquest in the magistrates' court at

Taverston and has read out the circumstances of Ben's drowning on 25 March in the miners' pool on Barrowdown. The formalities of identifying the body have been gone through; the pathologist has given his evidence along with the detective inspector, the constable and the school bus driver. A written statement given by two school-children has been read. Tom Band has satisfied the court he knows lying from truth and is in the witness box. Tom's normally ruddy face is very pale. He is wearing his school suit, and his hair has been smoothed flat with oil by his aunt, who is determined the Bands shall have nothing to be ashamed of. His tongue is tied with terror that something he may accidentally say will implicate his sister, who he believes guilty, though of what he is uncertain.

The coroner glances wistfully through the window at the spring sunshine, then, with an effort of will, blinkers his mind to concentrate on Tom.

'There are only a very few questions to ask you, Tom. I don't want you to become worried or anxious but simply to answer 'yes' or 'no' as I put the question to you.'

Tom's face remains without expression.

'I understand you returned from school on the school bus at four o'clock on 22 March?'

Tom looks around helplessly, he's no idea of dates.

'I dunno when it was.'

The coroner sees fit to supply the information.

'I can assure you it was 22 March. Did you return on the school bus that day?'

'Must've.'

'You came down the lane to the house as you always do on returning from school?'

'Yes.'

'Did you see anyone coming along the lane opposite?'

'No.'

'Yet people in the school bus saw someone running along the lane.'

In the silence that follows a tortoiseshell butterfly flutters frantically against the chapel-shaped window, tragically enmeshed in a spider's web the cleaner has failed to see.

'Did you see someone running along the lane, Tom?'

'No.'

'Think carefully. You didn't see your sister running along the lane?'

'No.'

The coroner sighs inwardly. There is nothing he hates more than an untruth uttered in one syllable. He makes a note.

'So you came through the farmyard and into your house. Into the kitchen?'

'Yes.'

'Was your sister there?'

Tom hesitates. 'No.'

'Was she upstairs, then?'

'I dunno.'

'You didn't go upstairs?'

'No.'

'So far as you know your sister wasn't in the house?'

Tom feels little drops of cold perspiration running down his armpit. He steadies himself on the shiny varnished Japanese oak box. His brain goes numb under tension, like in mental arithmetic at school.

'I heard her up above.'

'Ah, you *heard* her. How did you hear her?'

'Walkin' about.'

'Was she doing her washing, would you say?'

Tom wavers in uncertainty. 'No.'

'Not doing it upstairs in the bathroom?'

'No.'

'Your sister has told the police that she was upstairs on that evening washing her clothes when you came in.'

No sound but the butterfly and the hum of cars along the main street.

'How did you know she was upstairs?'

Tom's small bony knuckles grip the safe and solid wood. He feels himself cornered, sees before him Tamsin climbing up wooden steps with a hooded hangman, then

166

stepping boldly out into space until brought up short by the noose. He has seen it too often on the telly for capital punishment to be abolished from his imagination.

'I heard the plug run out.'

'You heard the bath-plug run out?'

Tom is convinced he's done it now: condemned Tamsin.

'Could your sister have been having a bath?'

'I dunno.'

The coroner continues to question Tom, but this is the best he elicits. Tom's evidence falls into doubt when he tells the court that he always knew his dad was up on Barrowdown because of his pendulum swinging over the map. The jury look at him curiously. If this is so, why did the boy not tell someone or go to see for himself? Tom cannot explain the dawning of his conviction, his apprehension, the feeling of disgust and revulsion, the dread of proving himself right, married to his obscure fear for Tamsin. So he stands obstinately silent. The jury decide privately that he is something of a village idiot. Tom leaves the witness box.

Rachel Band, for whom the coroner has delayed the inquest until she could be found, now comes in and takes his place. Rachel wears a smart dark suit and hat with one feather that curves around her cheek; a short veil covers her forehead. She is made up for Wandsworth, where she was finally located. As she stands in the box she removes her gloves and then puts them on again. London has not come up to expectations and now that the police have fetched her down she doesn't think she'll go back, not with Joe in the nick. She won't stay round this area, though, not with the stink Ben's gone and caused, no thank you. No hope of work if you were a fourth cousin, let alone his wife. She feels sorry for Tamsin, poor kid. One thing she has had is a glimpse of Tom, so there's never an ill wind that blows no one any good. Rachel is momentarily comforted. The coroner studies Rachel. Experience tells him she will at least talk, which will be a relief after the boy.

'Mrs Band, I understand that you used to work at

Asherford Garage until you became implicated in a theft of money from the till?'

'I was friendly with the person who took it, if that's what you mean.'

'And have continued to remain "friendly" with Joe Sanders until he was caught by the police in London and taken to serve a sentence for theft?'

'Yes.'

'You also asked your daughter to take money from her aunt's private desk to replace money you had "borrowed" from the till?'

'I asked her to take it as a loan. I was to pay it back.'

'And did you?'

'Not yet I haven't.'

The jury stirs. They would like to pin blame on this woman who has abandoned her children and run off with some good-for-nothing thief. The coroner presses Rachel with more questions, referring to her 'indiscriminate choice of men' until she bursts out:

'I needed the money, see. Ben was never any good. He drank. He never gave me nothing all those years, nor did his sister. She was behind it. She never let me see my own kiddies—'

The coroner interrupts. 'Mrs Band, could you please simply answer my questions.' He coughs and clears his throat. 'Tamsin Band walked over to you at Asherford on the night of 22 March. Did you know this?'

Rachel passes her tongue over her lips, enough to moisten them but not to remove her lipstick. They will shine brightly, belie the anxious beating of her heart.

'No.'

'You didn't see her when she arrived at Asherford on that night?'

'No.'

'Were you expecting her?'

'Not then, no.'

'But you were expecting her sometime?'

'No.'

'She wasn't by any chance planning on going to London with you?'

Rachel debates her answer only for a second, but it is enough for the coroner to surmise that 'no' will mean 'yes'.

'No,' Rachel answers.

'So it was just a chance, a surprise, that she came over on that particular night?'

'Yes.'

'You don't find it surprising?'

'Not if Tamsin wanted to see me, no. We'd been kept apart all those years.'

'Does it not suggest to you she must have been deeply disturbed by something?'

'I don't think she was very happy out Ventnor.'

The coroner continues to question Rachel at length. His tone, his attitude, all combine to convey to the jury that Rachel Band is a bad lot. And implicit in this assumption is the other: that Tamsin Band has her mother's blood in her and is likely to be no better.

Eventually, when Rachel leaves the box, she is replaced by Dora. The big clock at the back of the court jerks its hour hand forward. Time passes; only in this court does it appear to have come to a halt. Dora stands in the witness box in her bottle-green and black coat and woollen beret. She holds her handbag in front of her with both hands and waits. The questions start. Dora answers precisely and convincingly.

'On 22 March you took your accounts down to the inspector of taxes in Taverston, Miss Band – is that correct?'

'Yes.'

'When you returned, who was in the house?'

'Tom and Tamsin.'

'Was Tamsin in bed when you left, or on the couch?'

'On the couch downstairs. But she was up when I come in.'

'What did you say to her?'

'I said seeing as she was up, she could go out and cut me a cabbage.'

'And then?'

'She went out and never come back, not that night. She went down her mother's.'

'When did Tamsin return?'

'The following evening on the school bus.'

'In your opinion, Miss Band, was Tamsin well enough to walk to Asherford? Had she recovered from her fall down the stairs?'

'I couldn't say. She done it so she must've.'

The coroner drinks from the cool glass of water at his elbow. Despite the taste of chlorine, he prefers it to the moor water bottled by his wife from the heads of bubbling streams. On the last occasion, she filled it not quite at the head, and walking up a little further they found the flow divided by a dead sheep. The jury, he notices, are beginning to feel the hardness of oak. They shift their buttocks and recross their legs.

'Have you anything you would like to add, Miss Band?'

Dora tenses herself for what she is to say. She looks at the sea of faces in front of her. She has promised before the Lord to tell the truth, so she will. The Lord will give her the strength to speak out. He, like herself, sees that Tamsin must not shirk the part she has played in Ben's death, though exactly what that part may be . . .

The coroner coughs, taps his Parker pen on his notes. Dora, like Tom before her, grips the witness box.

'I found a bucket of wet clothes pushed behind the wardrobe in her bedroom – four days after, it was. They was beginning to get the mildew on them.'

'Tamsin's clothes?'

'Yes.'

The jury lean forward; this is new, certainly evident of something. Their wandering attention is brought back into focus.

'The ones she would have been wearing in your absence?'

'The ones she most likely put on when she got dressed.'

'Can you think of any reason for Tamsin to need to wash her clothes that day?'

'I'm sure I don't know why she wanted to.'

'Why do you suppose, Miss Band, that Tamsin did not put her clothes to dry.'

'I couldn't say.'

'Could it have been that she did not want anyone to know she was doing her washing?'

Silence. Dora's concentration has slipped away. She is uncertain what to answer. The coroner tries again.

'Why, Miss Band, should Tamsin have felt the need to conceal her washing?'

'She didn't want me to see it, I suppose.'

'Why didn't she want you to see it? Was it probable you would reprimand her on this occasion?'

Dora hesitates. 'I don't reckon she'd'a done it without a good cause.'

'What good cause do you suggest, Miss Band?'

The butterfly gives a last helpless flutter. The spider darts eagerly along the sill towards it, thinks better of its boldness, and retreats again.

'My guess is they was wet already.'

A spellbound silence.

'Wet? Why should they have been wet?'

'She'd been in the water, if you ask me.'

'Why do you say this, Miss Band?'

'There was mud on the bottom of the bath.'

At this point Dora happens to see the face of Dr Ash amongst the witnesses. There is something about his presence that prevents her speaking out further. Finally the frustrated coroner gives up.

'Thank you, Miss Band, that will be all for the present.'

Dora leaves the courtroom. She does not feel as absolved, as at ease, as she feels she should. The courtroom door opens and closes behind her.

The coroner refers to his notes, then looks down at the bench in front of him.

'Dr Ash, I believe you volunteered information to the police. May I now ask you about what you have said?'

Dr Ash gets up heavily and climbs into the box. He limps slightly, taking each step separately. His bald head has a few white hairs remaining on it. Immediately he speaks, everyone takes notice. His voice is authoritative, deep and firm. It implies both truth and accuracy, but who in such a case can be certain? Tamsin, outside, waiting with the others to be questioned, shrivels at the thought of the doctor's evidence. It is what she most dreads; the shame and humiliation. She prays he will say nothing. She would rather go to prison than that he should make public the darkest secrets of her being. She looks down and sees the nails of her right hand have pressed so hard into the palm of her left that blood shows.

'Doctor, I believe you visited Tamsin Band at her home on 19 March. What was the reason for this visit?'

'I received an emergency call saying the girl was unconscious.'

'Due to a fall down the stairs?'

'That came later.'

Can you describe your visit and the extent of the patient's injury?'

'Tamsin had recovered consciousness by the time I arrived – about twenty-five minutes after the call. She was suffering from shock and a blow on the side of the head.'

'What in your opinion caused the blow on the side of her head?'

'She almost certainly struck her head against something as she fell. Probably the bottom step of the staircase.'

'But you didn't think it necessary to take her into hospital?'

'No. Rest was all that was required. Tamsin has a strong constitution. I last saw her at her birth.'

A stir and murmur from the jury, almost laughter.

'So it doesn't surprise you she was able to walk to Asherford three days later?'

'No.'

The coroner eyes Dr Ash disbelievingly, and makes a note.

'Thank you, doctor. Is there anything further you would like to add?'

The doctor seems in two minds whether to leave the box or not. The faces round and beneath him wait expectantly. He thinks of Tamsin lying on the couch in Ventnor kitchen, the anxiety with which her eyes implored his silence. With an effort he puts her face out of his mind. The truth, as he sees it, must come first. If he had reported her condition, done his duty in the first place, Tamsin might well have been free of the suspicion that clings to her now like a too strong scent.

'I should like to say that I don't believe Tamsin Band ever fell down the stairs. I believe the blow on her head was caused as a result of a blow on the head from the other side, and was almost certainly inflicted by the same person who caused injury to her body.'

For a few moments the court is completely silent until one of the jury drops a biro which clatters and rolls behind their bench.

'Please clarify your statement, doctor.'

'I am suggesting Tamsin had been physically punished to the extent of assault and bodily harm . . .'

Dr Ash goes on to describe the welts he found on Tamsin's body during his check-up.

'Yet you said nothing?'

'Neither Miss Band senior nor Tamsin made any claim. Both said any marks on her were due to her fall. There was nothing I could do except refer the case to a social worker, which in this instance I doubted would be of any benefit.'

'You are certain the marks you saw couldn't have been due to a severe fall?'

'I'm certain the welts were not due to a fall.'

'You mentioned assault, doctor. By this do you mean indecent assault?'

In the pause that follows the court waits breathlessly. In the public gallery Edith feels her entire body quivering from the tension. She wouldn't like to be Dora, oh no she wouldn't, but then the Bands have always been odd ones.

'I have no evidence to claim more than I have already stated.'

'Thank you, doctor.'

Dr Ash climbs out of the box as slowly and carefully as he has mounted it, and is replaced by Ron Band. Ron is wearing his market suit and gaiters. He feels stiff and uncomfortable, but then this is an uncomfortable business for Ron, because he must concentrate on not telling the truth and being consistent about it. For Ron, like Tom, intuitively feels it better not to have seen Tamsin running back along the lane on 22 March. So Ron places his well-scrubbed though dirt-ingrained hands on the edge of the witness box and studies their black hairs. It helps him to concentrate.

'I understand, Mr Band, you were up in the fields on the afternoon of 22 March. What kind of work was occupying you?'

'Lambing.'

'Delivering lambs?'

Ron hesitates – not from a wish to alter the fact, but from a desire to correct the term 'delivering'. As a description of helping with a birth it always seemed to him inappropriate, reminding him more of the baker or the postman, something done to order instead of the irregular heaves and spasms of pain he confronts every spring with his ewes.

The coroner becomes impatient. 'Was there something you were going to say?'

'No.'

'You were delivering lambs on that afternoon?'

Ron gives the briefest indication of assent.

'Where was your niece when you left the farmhouse?'

'Downstair – on the couch in the kitchen.'

'Would you have said she was ill?'

'Doctor told her to stay abed.'

'But you didn't consider her ill?'

174

'I reckon she must'a been, or doctor wouldn't'a telled her to stay abed.'

Ron Band is choosing to speak in far broader dialect than he would dream of using even amongst his own family. When having tea with Mrs Barnett, Ron's speech is very similar to her own.

'So then it was a surprise to you to see Tamsin running along the lane beneath you on that afternoon?'

'I never seen her.'

'Come, Mr Band, the lane was directly beneath the field in which you were seeing to your flock. If people from the bus passing along the opposite side of the valley could see someone moving, running, along the lane *and* you in the fields above, it seems unlikely that you could have missed her.'

'I never seen no one.'

Silence. The jury observe with interest the clash of wills. The coroner and Ron look at each other like fighting cocks.

'Mr Band, we have been told just now by your sister that Tamsin had a bucket of wet clothes behind her wardrobe. Does this not suggest to you that Tamsin must have been out during that day, that her clothes must have become muddy, or wet?'

'I couldn't tell you why she done it.'

'You can't in any sense account for the wet clothes?'

Ron thinks for some moments. The jury's collective mind wanders. He rubs the back of his neck.

'She must'a been an' done her washing.'

'Why should she then put it behind her wardrobe?'

'Very likely she didn't want Dora to know she'd been running off the hot water in the afternoon. Dora wouldn't'a been very pleased if she'd'a knowed.'

For the first time Ron Band looks up in some satisfaction. As Dora would say, the Lord was putting words in his mouth. The coroner says something confidential to his clerk and makes a note. He coughs and takes a drink of water.

'I understand from Dr Ash that he was called to the farm

three days earlier to examine Tamsin after a severe fall down the stairs?'

Ron nods – the kind of nod he habitually uses when bidding in the market.

'I'd be glad if you could answer "yes" or "no."'

Ron nods.

'And that the doctor discovered severe welts amounting to bodily harm?'

Ron nods.

'Your brother, I am told, was chastizing Tamsin for the theft of £50.'

'It weren't no theft. She was borrowing it for her mother.'

'Do you consider Tamsin might fancy herself over-punished, and for this reason might have borne a grudge against her father?'

'It's not for me to say.'

'Mr Band, I'm asking you a question. I expect an answer.'

'I reckon Ben overdone it. I don't reckon the girl would'a borne him no grudge.'

Although Ron's movements during that day have been confirmed by Mrs Barnett walking her dogs, another neighbour, and Wally White, he is questioned longer than any of the others except for Tamsin. The coroner assumes rightly that the truth on all counts can be got at through Ron, but Ron concentrates the full force of his able brain on protecting Tamsin. The coroner is as frustrated over obtaining truth from Ron as he would be were he to try digging a vein of gold from rock with a spade. Finally he calls for Tamsin Band.

Tamsin has got thinner in the last two weeks and in consequence looks taller as she stands in the witness box. Her eyes are like brown pools against the pallor of her skin; her dark hair has also grown longer and stretches down her back between her shoulder blades. She wears a white blouse with a high lace collar, and a plain skirt to beneath her knees that gives her an old-fashioned look. Has Tamsin chosen to look like this from conscious reasoning or from subconscious need, or is her appearance entirely due to her wearing her only best clothes? Whatever the reason, she stands now, waiting to be questioned, quite unconscious of the impression she makes. The only faces she recognizes in the room are those of the family solicitor, who will take her part in front of the coroner, and Dr Ash. Outside, with others of her family waiting to be questioned, she has seen her mother and has been able to speak to her briefly, although under the supervision of the police. Rachel has embraced Tamsin, covered her with kisses and also managed to murmur in her ear that Joe is in the nick. Tamsin supposes it was to be expected. It's a great relief to her that her mother is not shut up with him. She wonders whether she has lipstick on her cheek.

It felt like a bad dream, standing up before strangers with the coroner sitting opposite, or a film on the telly. I felt afraid. Before he began, he told me I was not bound to say anything that might incriminate me, then he started asking general questions about Ventnor and school until he gradually led round to what he wanted to know.

'I understand that on 22 March you were at home from school after a fall down the stairs two days earlier. Am I correct?'

'Yes.'

'That on the third day you were still recovering quietly in the house?'

I hesitated. 'Yes.'

'Were you in some doubt?'

'I went along the lane to see if there was any new lambs.'

'What time of day was that?'

'I don't know exactly.'

'About four p.m.?'

'Could've been.'

'Did you see the school bus?'

'No.'

'You're quite sure you didn't see it going along the road opposite?'

'I might've. I can't remember for sure. It goes along every day except weekends.'

'You saw the lambs, but not your uncle, who was lambing?'

'They were in the field the other side of the lane.'

Then you ran back along the lane. Why?'

'I didn't run.'

'People in the school bus saw you running.'

'Maybe I was. I don't remember.'

'Do you usually run for no good reason?'

'I was most likely cold.'

'How long were you out altogether, would you say?'

'About twenty minutes.'

'And that was the only time during the day you were out?'

'I went out that evening to get a cabbage for my aunt.'

'You not only went out that evening to get a cabbage for your aunt, as you tell us, but you walked most of eight miles to Asherford that night.'

There was a shift and stir from all of them listening.

'I got a lift,' I said.

'Indeed you did. We know about that. You arrived safely at the garage where your mother, Mrs Rachel Band, works – and to whom you had been paying regular visits over the last few weeks. But she apparently had left the place and you spent the night in a disused car.'

I could hear Edith start into a coughing fit up in the public gallery. I'd know that cough anywhere.

'Yes,' I said.

'I suggest, Miss Band, that neither your fall down the stairs nor any other injury you may have suffered was enough to deter you from taking a walk up to the miners' pool on that day, a short walk in comparison to your walk to Asherford.'

'I didn't go up there.'

'You are quite certain of this?'

178

'Yes.'

The coroner sat back, drummed his fingers on the desk and sighed. He said something to his clerk. For a moment I almost told them the truth, but fear stopped me. I reckoned they were trying to say I'd pushed Dad in, and how was I to prove I hadn't? If I'd kept quiet for all this time about seeing him, then that's what they'd think. They were bound to.

The coroner went on. He tried a different line.

'I apologize for the personal nature of some of the questions I am forced to ask, Miss Band, but if you can answer as clearly and directly as possible, it will save the necessity for prolonging my duty.'

He cleared his throat.

'Could it be that the welts on your person were not due to a fall down the stairs, but due to chastizement from your father?'

'No.'

'No? Can you explain what you mean?'

'I fell down the stairs.'

'Your father did not punish you or hit you for stealing £50?'

'I borrowed the £50.'

'So your father at no time laid a hand on your person?'

'No.'

'Yet the doctor is prepared to swear the welts on your body were caused by blows inflicted by another person.'

I didn't give any answer. The coroner wrote something down.

'Be that as it may, you were unwell enough to need a doctor and on the third day were still recovering in the house when your aunt went down to market?'

'Not down to market, down about the accounts.'

He made a correction in his notes. I think he felt he was making progress with me for he changed his voice to kind of carefully pleasant, like he might speak to a child.

'You remained in the house all day except for the one time you went out to see the lambs?'

179

'Yes.'

'Was it a nice day, can you remember?'

'Yes – sunny.'

'How do you know it was sunny if you didn't go out till late afternoon when the sun would have gone behind the ridge?'

'The sun came in the window.'

'The window in your farm kitchen where you were on the couch is on the north side of the house. In winter the sun wouldn't come in the kitchen.'

'I could see it on the slope of hill opposite and when I went upstairs.'

'To wash your clothes?'

'The toilet's upstairs.'

'But you were in the bathroom washing your clothes, or rinsing them, when your brother came back from school?'

'Yes.'

'Having washed your clothes, why did you put them, still wet, in a bucket behind the wardrobe?'

'I didn't want my aunt to know I'd been washing. She'd told me to stay in bed.'

'Why did your clothes *need* washing?'

I shrugged. 'It seemed like they did.'

I thought I heard the faintest murmur of sympathy from somewhere out in the court.

'So what did you envisage doing with the bucket of wet clothes?'

'Hanging them out on the line the next day when the doctor said I could get up.'

'But as it happened, you forgot them?'

'Yes.'

'Your story is not very credible to those of us listening.'

I stayed silent. I wished I knew what all the rest had said. Any moment I thought he was going to tell me Ron or Tom'd seen me coming back along the lane, running. My forehead was wet with sweat. I wiped it hoping no one would see, but they must have. There isn't much shelter when you're stood up in a witness box. He asked me a lot more questions, then at last it came:

'As I believe you know, Miss Band, you were seen running back along the lane between the moor and Ventnor farm at four o'clock on that afternoon by several people in the school bus – the same bus that your brother had just got off.'

'It wasn't me.'

'At least three people, including the driver, are prepared to swear it was.'

'It's too far off to see who it was.'

'That is open to debate.'

So it went on, more and more questions, him asking me all sorts, trying to force me into things I wasn't ever going to say. He kept harping back to my mother, my visits down there, Joe, and above all the £50. He wanted me to admit I'd taken it without permission, that, to put it plainly, I'd stolen it. I hated him. He made me sound like a thief, someone you couldn't trust; he twisted things round to make them out quite different. Some of the time, when there was a break, I wondered about Joe. I felt sorry for him in spite of everything. He was brought in as a thief and no-good, the kind of person my mother kept company with and whose influence I'd come under. It came out about him taking me home at nights though they didn't know all of it. I was sure my mother must know about me and Joe, and I guessed she wouldn't want any more to do with me. That was the thing that upset me most.

At last they let me go. I felt drained as anything.

The solicitor employed by Legal Aid to represent the Bands now puts forward all that is favourable for Tamsin Band. He emphasizes the naturalness of Tamsin's desire to become reacquainted with her mother. He stresses the reprehensible manner in which Rachel Band has been treated by Benjamin Band, that no provision of any sort was made for her after she had left the farm although she remained Ben's wife; nor was she allowed access to her children. On the contrary, for a long time they thought her dead. This situation has inevitably resulted in a lowering of her standards in order to provide for herself. He admits that Rachel has acted irresponsibly towards Tamsin, manipulating her to her own purpose. Tamsin, he says, is no more than a pawn in the hands of all the Bands, and her mother has taken particular advantage of this. He plays down the doctor's evidence. At all cost he doesn't want Tamsin to have a motive. Instead he points out Tamsin's loyalty to her father, a loyalty that bears him no resentment; even though her father chastized her for borrowing the money for her mother, Tamsin will stand by him, support him 'to the hilt'.

The solicitor pauses a moment, takes out a dark maroon handkerchief with a white and grey weld-mesh pattern, and pats his temples. He continues. He objects, he says, to the coroner's possibly mistaken inference that Tamsin has 'stolen' the £50, when clearly she has borrowed it from one member of the family for the other. He then alters his tone and talks of Benjamin Band's drinking bouts with sadness; he doesn't doubt that an excess of alcohol in the blood has been the cause of his 'shockingly sudden' death. The pathologist's testimony, he feels, is conclusive. Ben Band was a massive and exceedingly strong man, and whether or not Tamsin Band had been up to the Miners' Pool (and he sees no need to doubt her word that she has not) there is absolutely no possibility that she could have had any determining influence over her father's death, whether accidental or suicidal.

The solicitor's crescendo is reached; he now modifies his tone to a dying fall to mention that Tamsin has been saved from he-doesn't-care-to-think-what kind of a life only by the goodwill of her aunt, Dora Band, and the kindness of her uncle, Ronald Band. He takes out the maroon handkerchief once again, which sign the coroner sagely takes to mean he has finished, and thanks him.

The coroner himself must sum up, making clear his own

feelings over the whole unsatisfactory proceedings, and hope to get home for tea and the six-o'clock news. His mind dwells briefly on his wife, who will be waiting for him in their sitting room with the granite fireplace of imitation moorstone carefully cut by machines. He glances at the clock, which gives another desultory jerk forward of the hour hand as though it too has had enough. The coroner takes some water and speaks to his clerk. The clerk announces a few minutes' break; he then fetches the Bands, who have been waiting outside in the company of two police. He points to an empty bench where they duly sit, well spaced out: Rachel, a space, Tamsin and Tom, another space, Ron, then finally Dora. It is bad enough that she and Rachel must be in the same room, let alone sit on the same bench. The doctor and solicitor are in the bench behind, along with Wally White, who has had his big moment earlier in the day when asked to describe how he found the body of Ben Band. The Bands are unanimously silent. The doctor and solicitor talk to each other, but what they say is drowned by the buzz from the public gallery. The coroner clears his throat, calls for silence. The summing up of the inquest on the death of Benjamin Band begins. It lasts for forty-five minutes before the coroner gets to his final question.

'Members of my jury, I should like you to think carefully and decide from the evidence you have heard whether Benjamin Band died from death by accident, by suicide, or death by the hand of unknown persons. If you don't feel there is enough evidence to justify such a decision, you must declare an open verdict. I think it has become clear to all of us that he was a confirmed alcoholic and an unhappy and irresponsible man. We have also learnt from two of the family that he was a man of immense strength.

'I would suggest to you that you take into account the doctor's evidence and consider it for what it is worth; whether, for instance, Tamsin Band may have been mistreated by her father and in consequence carried a grudge against him. I would draw your attention to the fact that she was by no means ill on 22 March, even if the marks from her injuries of two days earlier remained, and that there is some doubt to her whereabouts during that afternoon; that she *would* have had time to visit the Miners' Pool and is claimed to have been seen on her return by the school bus. Although someone moving along the lane is verifiable from across the valley, their identity would not be; so we have no right to assume it was Tamsin Band. Under the circumstances it is a very great pity that the pathologist is not able to tell us, except within two or three days, the time of Ben Band's drowning. Had the body been discovered earlier it would have made our problem very much easier.

'Finally, I should like to say that I am asking you to bring to bear your judgement on an extremely difficult case, one in which the majority of witnesses are members of the Band family. The extent of their collusion, or lack of it, I must leave you to decide for yourselves. At the same time I have been struck by the contrary evidence we have heard and, in some cases, a lack of truthfulness that has become self-evident. I ask you now to adjourn for ten-minutes, to discuss carefully amongst yourselves . . .'

The coroner's voice drones on. He has ceased having to think. His instructions are now automatic, for he has repeated the same phrases many times before. The others must remain in court until the jury returns a verdict. The coroner hides a yawn. It has been a long and unsatisfactory day. The verdict any sane jury is bound to give is obvious, but in his experience juries are seldom sane. He abhors juries and considers them the perfect example of non-thought, non-logic; nor can he give them any credit for common sense. There is absolutely nothing to be said in their favour, as anyone who has worked much with them will agree. As he sees it, the use of a jury is where the entire system of law comes to grief. Trial by jury! God preserve him from ever being put before one in this world or the next. An image of a jury consisting of winged blondes comes before his mind's eye, causing him to shiver involuntarily and feel behind him to see if the radiator is on. How arbitrary, he reassures himself, all judgement is.

I was shaking, I couldn't stop myself. I don't know what I expected them to say but I was afraid. I don't think I've ever been more afraid than waiting for that jury to come back and give their verdict. I glanced along at my mother. She was pushing a stray piece of hair back under her hat. Tom, quite close on my right, was sitting on his hands and rocking, making the whole bench judder. Dora was sitting stiff and straight. Ron was bent forward looking at the floor, his hands gripped between his knees.

Then the door opened and the jury came back. They took a long time sitting down. Then the coroner asked them their decision. One man stood up and spoke for them all. They were all agreed, he said, on an open verdict. I suppose I should have felt relieved, but the truth of it was I was too dead scared of crying in front of everyone to feel anything. I was numb. I could hear the voices round, but it was just a buzzing noise.

There was one person did puzzle me for a long time after and that was Tom. By listening to the summing-up I knew he'd lied and I reckoned he was sure I'd had to do with it. I spent a lot of time guessing what he knew and what he thought. Finally I couldn't stand not knowing any longer and got him on his own when we were out in the buildings and I was certain Dora and Ron were in the house. I quizzed him good and proper.

'Why did you tell all of those lies, Tom?' I asked.

'What?' he said, thick like.

'You know,' I said. 'Saying you saw me on the settee and nothing about the bath nor seeing me coming back along the lane?'

Tom was over the partition so I couldn't see his face. I could hear by the way of the sucking the calf was getting its head low down the bucket.

'I dunno,' he said.

You can't talk with Tom. It's impossible.

'You must,' I said, 'or you wouldn't have done it.'

He didn't answer. The bucket clanked.

'Did you think Dad drowning was my doing?' I asked.

'Dunno,' he said, but I could tell he did.

'Well it wasn't,' I said. I was bent over keeping two calves back while a third got its head in the milk. I straightened up and looked over the partition down on Tom, who was squatted down in the straw.

'I found him the day you saw me,' I said.

'I know,' he said.

'How?'

'Pendulum,' he said.

'You're an idiot,' I said, annoyed; then, 'What else did it say?'

'It doesn't *say* nothing,' he said. 'Just goes round quicker.'

'Over where someone is?' I asked.

'Yep,' he said.

'So you knew where Dad was?' I said.

'Yep,' he said.

'How long did it say he was up there before I found him?' I asked, curious.

'Dunno. Day or two.'

'Why didn't you say?' I asked.

'I told 'em back in the court,' he said, 'but they didn't believe none of it.'

'You mean you knew Dad had drowned himself up there?'

Tom looked up, puzzled. 'No, I didn't know that. Not till that afternoon I seen you coming back.'

'How did you know then?' I couldn't let it go.

'Dunno,' he said.

'Dad was dead when I found him,' I said. 'Drowned. Do you believe me?'

He was thumping the calf's nose, trying to get it out of the empty bucket. He straightened up. He was getting

186

nearly as tall as me, I noticed. He looked at me over the partition, intense and reproachful.

'Course,' he said.

20 August 1975

'Tamsin Band?' she asked.

'Yes,' I said.

'That's right.' She made a tick in her diary or whatever. She closed it, sat back, crossed her leg and closed her hands over her knee. She had on blue tights and a dark red skirt. Her goldy red hair was straight and covered one side of her face. She seemed different altogether to the one who'd come down Ventnor. A fan went round on the ceiling.

'I've been asked to have a talk with you,' she said, ever so pleasant. 'I work in conjunction with Alice, who's the social worker in your area. And she, as well as your aunt and uncle, and your head teacher' – she smiled – 'thought I might be able to answer questions about careers, or generally give you advice about anything you want to know.'

I pushed myself round a bit in the chair. My chair was low and soft. It made me feel relaxed sitting there listening to her up above me on her swivel chair, turning now this way, now that, like a weathercock in a changing wind.

'Are you comfortable?' she asked.

'Yes,' I said. I was.

'Our main concern,' she said, 'is that owing to your father's death you've under-achieved in your 'O's, which is sad because the results give no indication of your real ability. Your school speak very highly of you. They have always thought of you as way above the average, and believe you could go on to the technical college and perhaps take your 'A' levels, should you want.'

She paused. I waited.

'But not with the 'O's you got last term. They, all of us, feel that if you can possibly face it you should sit them again. This autumn or next summer.'

I pushed myself forward to the edge of the chair. 'I

187

thought I'd go to London and get a job,' I said.

'Your aunt and uncle want you to stay at home for another year,' she said. 'Frankly, it does seem sensible.'

I didn't say anything. I looked at the pattern on the green linoleum at her feet.

'Are you hoping to join your mother in London?' she asked.

'I don't know,' I said.

'There's another thing we ought to talk about,' she said. 'The police mentioned it. Personally I can't see much point in bringing it up at this stage, but I have to. You see, they are not convinced you were always accurate in your statement. They feel it would have been better for you to have told them everything you possibly could, volunteered information, when you were questioned . . .'

I looked up at the heavy woman with the red-gold hair that had slipped forward to cover even more of her face. I could sense something I needed in her, a warmth I wasn't used to. But my dread of her authority barred me from cooperating with her. She was one side of the fence, I was the other.

'Do you want to talk to me about it? Sometimes it helps, you know – talking to someone outside the family. I am not an informer. Nothing you say to me will be told to anyone else. But it might help you to decide what you are going to do, and me to advise you.'

I looked at the light coming through the Venetian blind. Yes, I thought, it would be great to have someone to talk to outside the family, but not you. I dread you like my family have dreaded for generations those who claim the law on their side. You are one of them, and though I like you, long to tell you everything, I can't tell anyone ever about me and my father, so I'll always be lying for the rest of my life.

I was sure I was the only person who'd ever had anything like that happen. Our lectures at school didn't tell us the truth about people and sex, just showed us diagrams and junk that we knew already, and ended up with a lot of soft-pedalling about it being 'natural and beautiful'. Back at Ventnor we saw the animals on the farm but they weren't like humans – that's what we thought. We learnt a bit from the telly when my aunt didn't switch off; and from the 'girlie' mags. But in them it was more like with me and Joe, only Joe would have loved me for real and not gone off. I wondered if men ever did love women. *Love*, I mean. If they *knew* what it felt like to love without . . .

She was asking me for the second time. 'Why do you want to go to London, Tamsin?'

'I can't get a job round here,' I said, 'because of all that in the papers.'

'I do understand,' she said, looking at me kind of gentle. 'I am well aware that nothing should have got into the press, and that it did. To me it seems quite unforgivable.'

But there it had been, unforgivable or no, right down to my wet clothes gone mouldy behind the wardrobe.

'They think I did it,' I said.

She frowned. 'Did what?' Her forehead wrinkled, the side I could see of it.

'Pushed Dad,' I said.

'Only malicious and unthinking people would think so,' she said, 'and you know it's not true. The pathologist's report on the level of alcohol in your father's blood made the cause of his death clear enough.'

I knew, and so did everyone else who knew the Bands, that Dad ran on alcohol like a car runs on petrol, so the alcohol level didn't count for nothing to those who knew him.

'What seems sensible,' she said, 'is for you to stay at school for the present. It will be to your advantage later. You'll be able to get away from home in another year by having better qualifications.'

I said nothing.

'Give time a chance. In a year or so everyone outside the family will have forgotten your father's death; then it will all be much easier for you. The problem is how we are to persuade you to relax and enjoy school work again. If we could do that, we'd really be getting somewhere.'

I felt myself slipping back into the chair. Sun was shining on the arm from under the blind. It was quite hot.

'I don't like school any more,' I said.

She swung her dark red skirt round on the swivel chair and took up a biro.

'I'd like to go to my mother,' I said. 'That's why they've sent me to see you, isn't it? To talk me out of it.'

With her back to me, writing, she said, 'Don't you think it would be better to settle for your family for the time being, however difficult you find living at home? There's your brother too. It would be much better for him if you could stay a little longer. All that happened must have been very upsetting for him as well as you. He must need you even if he can't show it.'

A bluebottle had made a mistake and come in the slit of open window; it buzzed loudly all round the ceiling. She looked up. We both did.

'I object to bluebottles,' she said, 'when you think of all the filth they go in.'

Like Dad, I thought, lying by the pool. I wondered if magpies had come and pecked his eyes like they do a dead sheep's. None of us had seen him except Ron. They'd told us not to.

She looked at her watch. 'I'm afraid I've kept you longer than I should have,' she said. 'I've enjoyed talking. I mean it. Come again next week if you can on . . .' – she looked at her diary – 'Wednesday. Same time?'

'All right,' I muttered. It all seemed inevitable somehow. Like she said, it seemed hard on Tom if I went, me being the only one in his family he'd got left. Another thing, I didn't know where my mother was any longer and she probably didn't want me. After the inquest she had stayed round Taverston for a while and I'd seen her a couple of times, then I went down a third time a few weeks later and she'd gone. The people she was lodging with told me she'd said she was going back to London. I asked if she had left any message for me or any address, but no – nothing. Looking at the room she used was like looking at a patch of ground where a tent's been pitched: final somehow, and frightening. Maybe Joe had come out and she'd gone back to him. She never wrote. I felt low for a long time after.

But not for the social worker, not for anyone, was I going back in school. I'd had a dose of it when they made me go in to sit my 'Os' in the summer, made me face all of them with their curious faces, their whispering in corners. Even Karen had been different, I'd felt it, though she acted friendly as ever. Forget, they all said. But I wasn't going to forget – and all of them living round weren't going to either, least of all my aunt. In a way they were right because if it hadn't been for me Dad would still be alive, that's certain. Little by little it got to seem I'd been making a fuss over nothing, and that Dad hadn't been so dreadful, and I'd been imagining the half of it. The lies and the truth started getting mixed up even in my own mind. And quite suddenly – snap – the dream came back about Dad falling through the floor and me doing nothing to help.

Shirley Eskapa
The Secret Keeper

'Shirley Eskapa's *The Secret Keeper* is a psychological study of an eternal triangle, the difference being that the child stands in as the eyes for the mother. Set in the claustrophobic atmosphere of Geneva's expatriate society, it is gradually revealed that the absent mother is working through the son she appeared to have left behind in order to wreak her vengeance on the mistress. Ms Eskapa is excellent at evoking the hothouse atmosphere of international finance and in seeing into the mind of a confused adolescent' OVER 21

'Shirley Eskapa's handling of the boy's point of view through his secret diaries is convincing and perceptive – she tells a gripping story with deftness and considerable insight' MIRANDA SEYMOUR, THE TIMES

'I enjoyed it so much – a beautifully sharp description of Geneva life' H. R. F. KEATING

'Sophisticated and sharp-eyed' COMPANY

The Secret Keeper is a masterful study of suspense, emotion and the highly disturbing implications of a torrid love affair plus the disasters of parenthood. The story is as taut as a violin string, controlled, subtle and intense, dealing with the clever manipulations of loving and supposedly caring mothers' SUNDAY EXPRESS

'This is a sparse, economical book written in a style taut and clipped, admirably suited to its hidden tensions. To create character through a journal is tricky enough but to base the whole plot on the diary of a thirteen-year-old is little short of foolhardy. That Shirley Eskapa just about avoids the pitfalls of such a device is proof enough of her considerable self-assurance' LITERARY REVIEW